THE FISHERMAN'S PROMISE

OLIVIA SNOW

For my dad

1

ELLA

I thank the removal men, pass them a crate of beer to show my gratitude, and watch absentmindedly as they drive back to the city where I've spent most of my life. That isn't my home now; it probably never will be again.

I close my eyes and try to blink away the tears that are always threatening to fall. How has it come to this? Twelve months previously, I'd been riding high on the success of my debut novel - a historical romance story set in the Victorian era. It had been so well received that the small publishing house I'd worked with had eagerly asked me to sign a new contract with them for two more books.

At the time, I couldn't think of anything I wanted more. With the money they'd offered, I'd been able to give up my soul-destroying 9 to 5 and spend my days dedicated to doing what I enjoyed most in the world - writing. Yet now I could barely put pen to paper - or finger to keyboard.

I was sure every author had to make do with unstable readers - I refused to call this man a fan. I guessed it was part of the job and just something you had to deal with when you put yourself out there into the world. But it was worse than I'd expected. I'd gone from successful debut author to anxious wreck in the space of a few short months. He was never far away from me, probing at my shortcomings and insecurities every single day.

My mental health was shot, and, unable to get away from the constant messages and phone calls (how he'd found my personal number, I don't know!), I'd done what any sane person would have surely done. I'd logged onto the authors' Discord I use and clicked over to the author retreat listings. A new one had recently been uploaded for Whitby in North Yorkshire - a six-month rental period with cliff-top views. It sounded perfect. Knowing I needed to turn my life around, I'd booked both the cottage and a removal company without a second thought. Now, here I was.

My rental cottage overlooks the rocky coastline, and I breathe in the fresh sea air, marvelling at the spectacular view of the choppy waves just a stone's throw away. I watch the sun setting behind me in an orange and pink sky, reflecting off the water and creating a beautiful mosaic across the horizon. Seagulls chatter above me, and I roll my shoulders back, trying to encourage myself to relax. *He can't find you here,* I tell myself, willing myself to believe it.

I walk inside, into the cosy living room where boxes are strewn about everywhere and pull the cable out of the Wi-Fi box that had been set up prior to my arrival. If I have any chance of healing, I need a complete break from technology. That means no smartphone, no laptop, nothing that connects to the internet at all.

I open a few of the thick cardboard boxes, slightly damaged from the trip over here, revealing the old books and photographs I hadn't looked at in years but that I'd packed anyway.

After taking a few minutes to reminisce, I potter around in the small kitchen, setting the water on the stove to boil and selecting my favourite mug from a box that I'd clearly marked "open me first". With a cup of tea in hand, I kick my shoes off and sink into the thick cushions of the chaise longue in front of the fireplace. The old chaise longue was one of the few items of my mother's I'd kept when she died, and it comforted me in a way little else could. Its fibres were worn but somehow familiar, like an old friend.

For the first time in months, I feel safe - like I can finally let my guard down and take time to process everything that has happened over the past year. I could sit here for hours, listening to the sea crash against the rocks below and watching the gulls dive for their dinner from my window.

I know people will be wondering where I've gone. I'm supposed to meet with my publisher next week, and my best friend Jess has been checking in on me dutifully, so she'll be concerned. But I have no words of any use to show, and Jess needs to live her own life. She said she didn't mind taking care of me, but there came a point a few weeks back when she'd got angry with me and started to question why I couldn't just ignore him. Easier said than done. It's hard to explain what it's like unless you've lived through something similar, so the support groups online tell me anyway.

I'd visited Whitby and the surrounding areas of Staithes and Robin Hood's Bay as a child with my parents, and on my drive up here, I didn't feel like much had changed. The same whitewashed buildings, the same winding streets, and the same quaint, cobbled ways remained. It was like I'd stepped back in time.

The Yorkshire Coast is a sleepy location with little to do, but for me, that's the point. I need to be alone. I close my eyes and try to let the town wash over me. No technology means there's no one to bother me, but no distractions from my thoughts means I'm left with too much time to think. Things are so much easier when I manage to shut my brain down or numb myself with alcohol.

I pull a notebook and pen out of the box beside me, its flaps creaking as I prop it up, and try to think of something to write - something I can show my publisher the next time I speak to her. But I can't do it. My head immediately goes to a dark place, which is the opposite of what I've signed up for. Wire Historical wants sexy Victorian stories, not ruinous thrillers.

I sigh and close my eyes, willing sleep to take me. I know it's unrealistic to expect to wake up tomorrow and suddenly be cured, but for now, I need relief from the torment.

I drift off to sleep, the scent of the ocean on the breeze soothing me.

My eyelids are heavy as I wake up, and I struggle to focus on the room around me, almost forgetting where I am. It's still dark outside, but the sound of waves crashing on the rocks reminds me of my move. I sit up slowly, easing the familiar crick in my neck that comes with nights spent on the couch, and make a mental note to at least get my bed set up today.

I move to stand, desperate for a strong cup of coffee to bring some energy back into my being, and fumble around, feeling for a light switch. The early morning darkness doesn't bother me anymore - not like it used to when I was a kid. It's the only time I've felt peace over the last few months. The only time *he* would sleep, giving me a break from the relentless emails and phone calls, not to mention the constant tags on social media with more vitriol aimed at me.

I push the dark thoughts out of my mind and brush my hand along the textured wallpaper, finding the switch and flicking it on. The orange bulb bathes the front room in a dim, romantic glow. It's just bright enough to see my surroundings and encourages my eyes to wake up properly.

I search through the boxes on the floor, desperate to find the granular coffee I'd brought with me. Eventually, I see it and pull open a metal tin, inhaling its nutty aroma. Just what I need.

My coffee is cooling down as I walk back into the living room, and I hear the seagulls start their morning call. It was one of my favourite sounds as a kid, signalling that dawn was on the way.

I place my coffee down on an unopened box and stretch my limbs. Sofa sleep wasn't exactly comfortable, but I feel better than I have in a long time. Maybe this move really will be positive. I just hope that Jess and everyone else from my old life understands.

Only time will tell.

2

JAMES

I wander along the cobbled streets illuminated by the soft pre-dawn light, my footsteps echoing in the stillness of the early morning air. The street lamps have been snuffed out, and I can just make out the silhouette of the harbour in the distance - my destination.

I pass by the paperboys with their bulky bundles and the milkman carrying crates of glass bottles with quiet determination. They're the only other people awake at this time in the morning. Even the market stallholders have yet to rise from their slumber.

I smile to myself, savouring the peace of this moment before it gets snatched away by the incoming bustle of the day, the mild flu symptoms I've been experiencing for a couple of weeks momentarily forgotten.

When I left school at 16, I felt like I didn't have many options but to work on the fishing boats with my best mate Paul. My dad passed when I was a baby, and a university education wasn't for me. Fifteen years later and I feel content with my decision. The job was hard and honest, and it paid my bills and rent. Granted, it wasn't a professional job, and I still lived in my hometown, but there were worse ways to live.

I walk along the final stretch of road towards the harbour. I can see Paul there already, inspecting the boat's equipment to make sure we're ready to set out for the day. I hurry along, knowing he'll need my help loading the supplies and bait.

"Alright there, mate?" Paul shouts, and I see him waving, a huge grin on his face as I draw closer.

"Yes mate, you?" I reply. "What's got you so happy this early? The sun hasn't even come up yet."

"God, don't remind me," Paul frowns. "I can't wait for the sun to get nice an' hot. The cold's enough to freeze my balls off."

I laugh as I climb aboard the boat bringing the last of the supplies with me. We spend a few minutes manoeuvring the equipment onto the deck, making sure everything is securely fastened down and nothing will fall overboard or get in the way during the day. My breath condenses into cloudy puffs of white in the still morning air, and I shiver against the chill of the early hour.

"Excellent," Paul says as we secure the last of our supplies down. "Ready for a good day of fishing?"

"Definitely. Mackerel should be running today. Could be a good haul."

"That's the spirit! Let's make some money!"

As we pull away from the dock and head out to sea, the sun slowly rises into the sky, lighting the water with glowing ribbons of gold. I might not have planned to stay in Whitby when I was a kid, but it was hard to complain about with such gorgeous scenes like this a part of my everyday routine.

"So, you think it'll be mackerel all day today?" Paul asks, breaking me out of my thoughts.

I nod, "That's what the reports say. And the water's been unusually warm lately, perfect conditions for them."

"Awesome. Let's hope our lines lead us to success!"

I chat excitedly with Paul about the best spots to try for mackerel and what techniques we might use to lure them in, despite us almost always using the same method at this time of year. By the time we near the fishing grounds, my anticipation is high, and I'm eager to get started.

"You know what they say; the early bird catches the worm, or in our case, the mackerel," Paul jokes.

I laugh, "Or maybe the early bird catches the headache from all the bobbing around."

"Ha! Good one, I'll fetch you a bucket just in case," Paul replies.

The sun is just beginning to peek through the rolling clouds and reflect over the sea as we set up our baited long lines with a mixture of small fish and squid. We exchange a knowing look as we make our way to the stern of the small commercial vessel, already feeling the anticipation of the day's catch in the air. We cast out our lines and watch them arc gracefully through the glassy surface of the water, the only boat in sight.

"That's the last of it," Paul sighs with relief as he drops the last line. "I hope we get a good catch. Could do with some money to put towards my wedding."

"Me too," I reply. "Still waiting for my invitation to be best man. How far along has she got with the guest list?"

"Oh, you know Beth," Paul laughs. "One minute, she's happy for it to be a small thing with a couple of witnesses. Next, she wants a full beach wedding with half the town in attendance. I'm just leaving her to it. She's happy, and that's the main thing."

I start the boat's motor and slowly move it through the water, allowing the lines to soak and the bait to attract the fish. "Well, as long as you don't leave me off the invite list," I jest.

"As if I would. Beth wouldn't let me! So, what's the plan for when we're done here today?" Paul asks. "Still coming to football practice tonight, I hope?"

"When have I ever not come, eh? It's the only night we do anything semi-productive," I laugh.

Most of my evenings were spent sitting in the local pub before returning home with fish and chips or a curry. I really needed to get out more.

"Yeah, we should probably do something about that," Paul ribs.

"We need to find you a girl. Beth's been going on about this new barista who's started working at the coffee shop. Maybe I could set up another little blind date for you? Ask Beth to tell her how amazing you are and all that."

I frown. It's not that I don't appreciate Paul's help, but the last blind date he set me up on didn't exactly go all that well. The girl was ten years my junior and had a fish phobia - there was literally no way of moving past that with my line of work.

"Nah, I'm good," I reply. "I'll meet someone when the time is right. Besides, knowing you, you'll set me up with someone completely incompatible again anyway."

"I still think you could have worked something out with that girl who was afraid of fish," Paul teases.

"Not with my work schedule," I frown. "Clothes that smell of fish and early wakeups aren't exactly a turn-on, are they?"

"Hey, I did find Beth, didn't I?"

"Yep, and you'd better keep hold of her. Ain't no way you'd find someone as amazing as her again."

We continue chatting and joking in the way only old friends can as we wait for the bait to attract the mackerel. Our lines quietly bob in the water behind the boat, and I can't see any other vessels even starting to head our way.

A few hours pass, and I kill the boat's motor, ready to see what delights the North Sea has provided for us today.

"Ready mate?" Paul asks.

"Ready," I confirm.

Paul and I take a winch each and start to pull in the lines. The boat rocks back and forth in the water, and it takes a moment before we steady ourselves. The cold, salty smell of the sea is heavy in my nostrils as I pull the first hook.

"We've caught a bounty!" Paul declares, throwing his fist into the air.

His enthusiasm is infectious, and I can't help but smile. A catch like this every day would be incredible. Fortune is clearly shining on us.

I stun the first fish I pull up before throwing it into a plastic container filled with ice, then do the same with the rest of them while Paul works alongside me. We've done this so many times now that we operate almost on autopilot, managing to do the work of four people between just the two of us.

With the crates fully secured, Paul starts the boat's motor again, and we head back to the harbour. Our boat is heavy with today's catch, and I can't help but feel proud of what we've accomplished.

"Man, what a day we've had out there!" I say. "The sea was rough, but we caught some big ones!"

"Yeah, and just in time for the fish market in town. These mackerel are going to fetch a pretty penny."

"Yep, I've got a feeling we're going to make a killing today," I add. "And I'm starving. I could go for a good plate of fish and chips to celebrate. Fancy it?"

Paul laughs. "Ha! You and your fish and chips. You could eat it every day and never get tired of it."

The morning sun shines bright across the still harbour as our boat chugs toward the docks. As we draw closer, the clamour of the morning rush grows louder. Tourists wearing light jackets and baseball caps amble along the pavements, admiring the shops and cafes on either side.

I watch the children sitting alongside the barriers, holding on tight to their fishing nets and buckets, excitement clear on their faces. Boats come in and out, and the air is filled with the sounds of seagulls, the lapping of waves, and the cries of the fishmongers.

"Well, here we are," says Paul. "Let's get these fish offloaded and get to the market. We've got a lot of work to do!"

I nod in agreement. "Agreed. It's going to be a busy day, but I wouldn't have it any other way!"

I bend down to grab the first heavy plastic crate laden with mackerel and feel a sudden, crippling cramp surge through my abdomen. I try to steady myself, but a sharp gasp escapes my lips, and my grip on the box loosens. Paul glances at me from the corner of his eye; his eyebrows creased in concern.

"You okay there, mate?" he asks. "Don't tell me you had another dodgy curry last night. I told you to stop eating at Tandoori Palace. You get food poisoning from there way too often."

I brush it off with a chuckle, though I still feel a dull ache in my side.

"It's the only place still open on a Monday night," I reply, trying to make light of the situation.

I bend down again, ignoring the pain. The box's corners dig into my sore hands, and I ignore the wave of nausea I feel as I carry it off the boat onto solid land.

I barely make it a few steps before the box crashes to the floor, and I double over so violently that I think I'm going to vomit.

Paul rushes to my aid and pulls me back into a standing position. "I'll take that," he says, relieving me of the weight in my hands, and I'm both embarrassed and thankful. "Dodgy curry or not, I'd get yourself home."

"Yeah," I mutter, holding onto my side. "You're right. Not sure what's wrong with me." I give him a quick nod and watch as he juggles the crates of fish over to a trolley.

I push through the sea of people, their conversations and laughter washing over me as I walk to a bench and sink down, my chest heaving. I watch as a lonely seagull flies overhead, its mournful cries blending with the cacophony of the street.

It couldn't have been a dodgy curry as Paul had suggested, as I'd enjoyed a bachelor-style meal of Pot Noodle after our night out the previous evening.

It's probably just a bad stitch. Nothing to worry about.

3

ELLA

I spend the morning unpacking boxes and building my bed. The bed frame is beautiful, but the instructions are as clear as mud, and I curse the fact that I've never found a man to help me with DIY. Despite having the instructions, I'm utterly clueless when it comes to construction. Still, it's finally done, and that means I won't have to spend any more nights on the couch.

I finish the job by folding the final corner of the quilt my mum had made for me when I was a little girl. I fondly remember her pulling the pastel shades of blue and sea green through the fabric and spreading it out on the standing frame for me to inspect. It fits perfectly across the double duvet, just like I remembered. The calming blues remind me of a peaceful ocean, which feels fitting for my new location.

My stomach growls, and I glance at my watch—2 pm. An empty refrigerator and nothing but a small jar of coffee, a crumpled box of tea bags and a few leftover shortbread biscuits in the cupboard are all I have in my new home. A twinge of guilt shoots through me—my mother's voice echoing in my ear, scolding me for not taking better care of myself.

I'm trying, Mum I reply with a desperate plea, the quilt reminding me she's never far away.

I sigh heavily and walk back into the front room, grabbing my purse, car keys and coat. It's time to venture into Whitby and pick up a few essentials.

I climb into my old trusty Vauxhall Corsa and shut the door behind me. Not long after I'd received my first royalty cheque, Jess had encouraged me to upgrade to a newer model. But I'd squashed her encouragement. My old car felt safe, and it was one of the few things even now that could offer me that.

I turn the key in the ignition, wrap my fingers around the steering wheel, and set off. The engine roars to life, dispelling the quiet around me as I ease onto the dirt track that winds away from my cottage, heading for the main road leading into town. As I drive, I glance around at the grassy hillsides dotted with wildflowers, and a rare shiver of happiness runs through me. I have never felt such contentment at being so utterly alone.

I park my car in the gravel lot near the bridge that separates the old, cobbled part of Whitby from its more modern counterpart and step out of my car, drinking in the nostalgia as I make my way to the marketplace. The air is filled with the sound of laughter and the scent of freshly cooked food. Everywhere I walk, from the colourful stalls selling tourist tat to the fish and chip van on one corner, feels exactly the same as it had when I was a child.

I take a deep breath, the noise of the marketplace and the familiar sound of bargaining beginning to overwhelm me, and look around the stalls. I make my way towards the centre until I spot a greengrocer with colourful fruits and vegetables stacked in neat pyramids.

"Good afternoon, love," the stall owner calls out in his thick Yorkshire accent as he spots me. "Let me tempt you in with some of this delicious veg!"

I nod, my stomach growling at the thought of a warm, hearty meal. He shows me some ripe tomatoes, potatoes and onions before carefully placing them into my basket.

"What else can I get you?" he asks with a knowing glint in his eye.

"This corn is particularly fresh today - perfect for adding to your dinner tonight."

"That sounds great," I reply, relieved at how easy this is. I'd hardly left the house towards the end of my time in the city - surviving on the odd pizza delivery whenever I could force myself to eat - and I definitely wouldn't have purchased food from anyone I had to talk to. The man grins before selecting some more items for me - peppers, mushrooms and aubergines - until my basket is full.

"How much do I owe you?" I ask him hesitantly, hoping I've brought enough cash to cover everything.

The man looks up from weighing my aubergine and smiles kindly at me. "That'll be twelve pounds, my love," he says. "Best fruit and veg in Whitby here. You make sure to come back now, you hear me?"

I smile and pass over some coins, thanking him for his generosity.

I hesitate before taking a few more careful steps around the marketplace. The bustle of people, smells, and sounds seem ever-growing, and I can't help but feel uncomfortable, like I'm being watched. As I walk past the fish stall, the seller notices me. He's wearing a thick red-and-white striped apron and a leather cap with a hook in it. I'm startled as he raises his arm in the air and waves with enthusiasm.

"Oi! Lady!" His voice carries over the bustle of the market. "If you like fresh fish, you'll love our mackerel - caught just this morning!"

He points to a tray of fish at his feet, gleaming silver in the light. I can't help but chuckle and walk over to him.

"Alright. Fish does sound good," I smile, pushing the dark thoughts to the back of my mind once again. *Nobody knows you're here, Ella; stop panicking.*

The seller grins broadly as he reaches for a gleaming silver fish from a pile beside him. "Look at that beauty!" he exclaims proudly before carefully placing it into a paper bag for me. He passes it across with a piece of lemon and some parsley before wishing me luck with my dinner tonight.

"Thanks so much," I reply gratefully.

The shopping basket in my hand strains at the seams, nearly

overflowing with my provisions. But despite the heavy load, a smile spreads across my face as I make my way back to the car. A strange lightness lifts my spirit for the first time in months, and I feel proud of myself for making it out of the house and visiting somewhere busy.

Moving was a good decision, I tell myself, believing it for the first time since I'd booked the cottage.

Just then, I spot a small independent coffee shop tucked away in a quiet side street. The scent of roasted coffee beans and sweet pastries wafts out from the entrance, coaxing me closer with every step. My mouth begins to water, and I find my stomach gurgling impatiently. *A warm pastry would be nice,* I think as I look inside.

The bell at the top of the door jingles as I enter, and I'm greeted by a warm and inviting atmosphere. A short, elderly man with diminishing hair and a checked shirt sits next to the window with his wife, while a young man with jet-black hair sits by the counter nursing what looks like a cold frappe. My favourite!

"Hello!" the shop owner calls out as I walk towards the counter. The young man looks at me and smiles, and I once again feel at ease. It's amazing how friendly the locals are here compared to where I'm from, and I also can't help but notice how good-looking he is!

My thoughts drift back to the last time I'd worked in the city. The flurry of suits with ties wound tightly around their necks, women walking head down with electronic devices in hand and bright red lipstick seeping through their smiles. It was a lonely existence.

"Hello," I reply, and both the barista and the man with jet-black hair smile warmly at me. "What a gorgeous coffee shop!"

"Thanks," the barista replies. She looks really pleased with my compliment, and I can't help but wonder if she's the owner of this quaint place. If the food is as good as the atmosphere, I could easily see this becoming my local. It looks like the perfect place to sit and write, and it's so down to earth compared to what I've been used to.

"What can I get you? A cinnamon bun, perhaps, or a ham and cheese toastie? I can warm one up for you; it's cooler than it looks outside!"

Both sound delicious. "I'll take a toastie and whatever it is that he's drinking," I say, motioning to the man beside me.

"Aha, you have another taker for the caramel special," the man says, a grin widening on his face. "I can't get enough of them. Beth here has a secret recipe that she refuses to share, so I have to keep coming back and giving her my money."

I can't help but laugh.

"Excellent. One caramel special and one delicious ham and cheese toastie coming up!" Beth says, and I watch as she busies herself behind the counter, her hips swaying as she walks.

She stops for a moment to talk to the man sitting at the counter while the toastie machine is working. I don't mean to listen in on their conversation, but the cafe is too small for me to give them any privacy. I guess this is the downside of not carrying a smartphone everywhere with you. I'd feel way less awkward if I could just put my headphones in.

"Are you sure you're going to be okay, James?" Beth asks.

"Yeah, promise, must have just pulled it on that crate, you know? They're heavier than they look."

I watch as Beth looks back to check on my toastie. Not yet warm, she carries on talking.

"I'm always telling Paul to be careful," she says, concern creased on her brow. "Just take care of yourself, ok? Get a hot water bottle or put some ice on it when you get home."

James smiles, the wrinkles around his eyes crinkling. "Thanks, Beth," he replies. "Let Paul know I won't be at football tonight, yeah? I don't want to let the side down".

Beth chuckles, her dimples deepening. I watch as her gaze shifts to the toastie machine, and my warm sandwich flops out. I glance away, feeling slightly awkward.

"Here you go! One ham and cheese toastie, just the way my regulars like it, and an ice-cold caramel frappe with extra whipped cream and chocolate shavings," Beth says, winking at me.

"Oi, how come I didn't get any chocolate shavings?" James laughs, and she pushes his arm.

"You're not a new customer, are you," Beth replies. "Gotta encourage this lovely lady to come back now, haven't I?"

"It smells delicious," I reply, smiling. I take the sandwich from her and wipe my hands on a napkin. "I'm Ella, by the way."

"Beth," the barista replies. "And this here is James." The young man smiles and performs a funny wave with his left hand as I pass some coins over to pay for my lunch, making me laugh.

I thank her again, carry my toastie and caramel frappe over to a table in the corner, and finally relax my heavy shopping bag on the floor.

My heart really does feel light, and as I tuck into my sandwich, a peculiar feeling washes over me. I'm not sure how to describe it, but despite none of the people I've met today knowing me, they've all greeted me with warmth. It's a welcome change from the constant horrid emails I've had sapping my confidence for the last few months.

Sounds of laughter echo from the counter where James and Beth stand talking, and I watch as the elderly man sitting near the window carefully wipes a crumb from his wife's mouth. It's such a lovely feeling to sit in public surrounded by so much love.

I WAKE the following morning with a full stomach and an optimistic outlook. The mackerel I'd had for dinner the night before was delicious, and I'd saved just enough to have it again for breakfast this morning. It again brought back memories of my childhood, of eating smoked fish with my dad while walking across the harbour. I decide that once I've done a bit more unpacking, I'll take a walk down there myself and try to remind myself of happier times.

I also make the decision to phone Jess. I'll need to turn my smartphone on to retrieve her number, but it will be worth it. I don't want her to worry about me, and I've been AWOL for a full 48 hours now. Hopefully, once she hears from me, she'll agree that I've made the best decision. Plus, she grew up in Whitby, so maybe she'll be up for visiting me for the odd long weekend.

By the time I drive into town and park up, I've managed to unpack almost all of my belongings. My rental house is looking somewhat like a home, and I'm starving.

The scent of fried fish and salty chips wafts through the air, and my mouth instantly begins to water. I rush across the street to the chippy and feel a wave of warmth as I pull open the greasy glass door. Inside, I can hear the sizzle of potatoes in hot oil and see the stacks of newspapers just waiting to be filled with delicious food. I place an order for a small portion of fish and chips to take away, the grease-soaked paper package warming my hands as I venture towards the harbour.

I sit down on a weathered wooden bench, looking out at the fishing boats returning from their morning expeditions. I open my lunch and can't help but chuckle as a bold seagull swoops in to try and steal a chip. It beats its wings determinedly and caws angrily when I shoo it away.

I squint against the bright afternoon sun and watch as two small fishing boats bob up and down in the calm harbour waters. I recognise the tall, broad-shouldered silhouette at the bow of one, and my heart skips a beat. It's the man who was sitting at the counter in the coffee shop yesterday.

He looks in my direction, and for a moment, I'm left wondering if he's talking about me. I watch again as he talks to the man beside him on the boat and points in my direction. After a short conversation, he turns, jogs across the gangplank, and seems to be heading towards me.

My heart rate quickens, and I can't help but feel a little bit excited.

4

JAMES

"Have you seen that girl before?" I ask Paul as we set about unloading the boat with our catch from today. I'd only seen her myself for the first time yesterday, and what did you know if she wasn't sitting eating my favourite lunchtime treat while watching the boats coming in.

"Nope, don't think so," Paul squints in the direction I point, trying to make her out. "Why?"

I can see her looking over at us now. We weren't half making it obvious.

"No reason," I reply. But I'm intrigued. She could have been a tourist, true enough, but most tourists only came to Whitby on the weekends at this time of year, so I had a feeling she might have been staying here more permanently. Only one way to find out, eh?

"Don't tell me. You like her, don't you? Our James is finally showing an interest in someone for the first time since 'fishgate2021'" Paul ribs me and literally does an air quote to emphasise his point. I can't help but laugh.

"Maybe I do, and maybe I don't," I reply, not wanting to give too much away. But it's Paul; he's known me most of my life, he knows I'm interested.

"Go and talk to her mate," he encourages. "I can handle the crates for today. It didn't take me that long yesterday, as it turns out. Just proves which one of us has all the muscle." He winks at me in an exaggerated fashion, half making me want to slap him over the head in response.

I don't hang around for him to change his mind, though, or offer me any more words of Paul wisdom.

My heart races as I get closer to her, and I can't stop myself from waving. She glances at me quickly and then looks away, tucking a strand of hair behind her ear as her cheeks fill with a blush. The anticipation of the conversation makes me smile; something about this girl has intrigued me.

"Hi," I say as I get close.

She looks up at me again with an apprehensive look, a look that I'm used to seeing from women on the rare times I find them attractive enough to be brave enough to initiate a conversation. I'm not bad looking, so I'm probably giving off really nervous energy. *Really off-putting, James; stop it.*

"Hello," she replies, and I listen carefully for any hints in her accent that may give away her origins. It's neutral, I think. Whatever, that hint of a northern lilt in her voice is sexy as hell. "Did you come over just to say that?"

"No." My stomach fills with butterflies as she speaks to me, more than I could have imagined under these circumstances anyway. "I saw you looking over at the boats and was sure I recognised you from the cafe yesterday. You're Ella, right?"

"I am," she smiles. "And you're James?"

"Got it in one," I laugh, glad she remembers me. "Look, I know this might seem a bit forward, but I got the impression you're new to the town, and I wondered if you might fancy joining me for a walk along the beach later? It's gorgeous in the evenings, and it's something you have to experience at least once while you're here."

I watch as she nervously fingers the edge of the newspaper containing her food, hiding her partially eaten fish and chips beneath her fingertips. "I, um, appreciate the offer, but I'm not sure that's a great idea right now. I-".

My stomach falls. I knew it was too good to be true.

"It doesn't have to mean anything," I say, hoping my voice doesn't sound as desperate as I feel. "I just, well, this sounds corny as hell, but I'm just gonna go with it. I'm a nice guy, honestly. And I feel like it is my duty to show every newcomer to the town a beautiful sunset."

"That sounds incredibly cliche," Ella laughs, and her smile lights up her whole face. She has the kind of beauty that could stop a person in their tracks.

"It sure does," I laugh, a little bit embarrassed.

"And you're right; I am new here. I only got here on Sunday, but I plan on sticking around for a while."

I watch Ella as she looks out over the boats bobbing on the harbour and the seagulls diving at unsuspecting tourists. She's so hard to read; I need to know more.

"What made you choose Whitby?" I ask her. I try to keep my voice steady, but I can't help but feel excited. This isn't the most glamorous of places, but to me, Whitby has always been the home of romance - cold nights walking on the beach, starry skies, and maybe a song or two played on the worn-out piano in the local bar.

"I was just stopping for a change of scene, really," she replies, continuing to look around at her new surroundings. "I wanted to move somewhere quiet for a few months to try and make some headway with a novel I'm writing. My best friend grew up here, and she's always going on about how she misses the quiet way of life. So, I guess I just thought I'd give it a go."

"There's nowhere better," I reply. "You'll not find a more stunning view anywhere in Yorkshire than from Church Hill."

She beams back at me and looks over at the Abbey, forever standing in the distance, looking out over the town.

"So, is that what you do for a living?" she asks, pointing to where I'd stood with Paul not ten minutes earlier. "Work on the fishing boats, I mean."

"Yeah," I answer with a smile, happy she wants to chat. "Me and

Paul run the boat together. His fiancée Beth owns the coffee shop you came to yesterday." I smile as I think about them. Those two are so in love that it's hard not to notice.

"Small world," she replies.

"We all grew up here, so we know this town and its people like the back of our hands," I say. "We've watched it grow over the years, seen businesses come and go. No matter how much changes, this place will always have a special place in our hearts. It's home!"

I take a deep breath and gaze out towards the horizon. I've never met anyone I've been attracted to as much as her before.

"That sounds wonderful," Ella replies, looking out to sea. "It must have been lovely to grow up here."

For the first time since we met, she turns to look right at me and holds my gaze for a moment. It's like an electric current passing between us, and I can feel my heart racing.

"So, what do you say? Want to give that beach walk a try?" I ask, holding my breath as I wait for her answer.

She smiles, and the sun sparkles in her eyes. "Yes," she says quietly. "I'd like that."

A faint blush creeps across my cheeks as I feel an unfamiliar warmth radiating from my chest. I can't take my eyes off her, and I find myself smiling despite my best attempts at a poker face.

"Great," I say, feeling a little giddy at the thought of getting to know her better. "It's a date then."

"Not a date," she admonishes. "Just two people checking out the beautiful sunset you promised me."

"Excellent," I reply. "Meet you by the whale bones in, say, four hours?"

"Sure," she laughs. "Do I need to dress for the cold or?"

"Yeah, I would. It can get a bit nippy down on the beach this time of year. It'll be worth it, though, I promise!"

We say our goodbyes, and I have a real skip in my step as I walk back to the fishing boats to finish helping Paul. He's nearly finished unloading all the crates by the time I return.

"Now then mate, looks like you had a decent conversation there," Paul jests as I bend down to help him with the final crate.

I grin, unable to keep the smile off my face. "Watching us, were you? Yeah, she's agreed to meet me for a walk along the beach tonight," I say.

"Oooh, very romantic," Paul ribs.

"Stop it," I laugh. "It's not a date. I just asked if I could show her around a bit. She's new in town and needs a knight in shining armour to show her all the best places and those best avoided."

"Knight that stinks of fish," he laughs.

"You wait," I reply. "If this goes well, you and Beth can stop carting me around like a lost puppy all the time. It would be good to invite someone new on our nights out, wouldn't it?"

Paul laughs. "I'm only jesting with you, mate. No need to justify yourself."

I finish helping Paul with the last of our catch and walk home with a big smile on my face, barely noticing the people and cars rushing past. My stomach flutters with excitement, and my palms are unusually sweaty. Every step I take feels lighter than air, the conversation I had with Ella replaying through my mind; her long auburn hair that cascaded over her shoulders, her gorgeous smile that lit up her whole face, and the sharp curves of her hips as she threw her leftovers into a bin and walked away.

A few hours later and I've bathed and dressed in an outfit that not only looks good but, more importantly, doesn't smell of fish. I've slicked my hair back with some gel, sprayed a spritz or two of aftershave on, and I'm fully ready to show this woman just how much of a catch I am. I still feel a bit shitty from the cold that refuses to vacate my body, but nothing's going to stop me from giving Ella a great evening.

I grab my car keys and drive the short distance through town to the whalebone statue that overlooks the seafront. As I park up and climb out of my car, I see her standing there, waiting for me.

I wave, a flicker of excitement running through my veins. I quickly lock the car and run over to her, a massive grin on my face.

"You came!" I say, not quite sure why I sound so surprised.

"Of course," she smiles. "I was promised a walk across the beach at sunset. What kind of woman would turn down an offer like that?"

I love her sarcasm and the way she makes me feel instantly at ease.

"Right then. Well, we'd better get down there," I say, grabbing her hand and pulling her along the promenade.

We make our way down the cobbled slope that leads towards the beach. Dusk is just beginning to set over the town, and there's hardly anybody on the beach now aside from the odd dog walker in the distance.

The sea air is cold, and a blustery wind whips through the air, which will hopefully lead to a spectacular sunset before long. We skirt past the rock pools and make our way down to the sea line, making sure to avoid the numerous rock landslides that have washed up on the beach from time to time. As we reach the sand again, the wind dies away, and the sea begins to shimmer in the last of the daylight.

"What do you think?" I say, turning to Ella. "Isn't it beautiful?"

"It really is. I've never seen anything like it. The sunset looks spectacular over the waves."

"Told you you wouldn't want to miss it."

Ella is quiet for a moment, and I watch her as she ponders what to say. Her eyes seem to twinkle as the last of the sun's rays hit them, and I can't help but marvel at her beauty. She notices me looking at her and smiles.

"I'm so glad I agreed to this," she says, reaching for my hand and squeezing it tightly. Her touch sends a shiver of excitement through me, and I can't help but want to know everything about this girl. "You're so lucky to live here."

"Are you planning on staying?" I ask her, hope running through me. "This could be something you get to enjoy daily if you do. And let's not forget Beth's frappes - I'll never be able to leave this town purely because I'd be unable to live without them in my life."

She squeezes my hand again. "I'm not quite sure just yet. I've rented a cottage until October, so I guess I'll have to see what happens between now and then. But you do make a compelling point with the frappes."

"You're here to write, right?" I ask. "Can you complete a novel that quickly?"

"My first novel took me the best part of a year," she responds, a darkness seeming to settle over her features. "But the publishing company I'm signed on with thinks I can do my next book faster, seeing as I don't have to work a day job alongside it this time. Not that I've managed to even start it yet..." she trails off.

"Well, hopefully the beauty of this place will help to inspire you," I say, knowing without a doubt that there can't be any more beautiful sights than the one we're both experiencing right now.

The sky around us has turned to an array of warm oranges, pinks and purples, all gradually fading away as darkness falls across the beautiful scene before us. We stand in comfortable silence, watching until finally, we are swallowed by nightfall—just two dots amongst countless stars twinkling above us like tiny pinpricks on a black velvet cloth.

The serene atmosphere is broken only by Ella's breathing, and as I look at her face, I notice tears running from her eyes.

"What is it?" I ask, using my thumb to wipe her tears away. "Is something wrong?"

"No," she replies. "It's just been so long since I've experienced something like this. Thank you for bringing me here tonight."

I wrap my arm around her and let her rest her head on my shoulder. Ella sinks into my body and looks out at the sea with the most mesmerised expression, and I can tell she loves being here just as much as I do.

We stand rooted in the same spot until we're surrounded by darkness. When I can no longer see the sea, I take her hand and lead her back to the promenade.

"Do you have any plans for tomorrow evening?" I ask her as we walk. "There's a lovely little bookshop café on Church Street that opens late on Wednesdays that I've wanted to try out for ages. It only opened last year, but they do some great home-cooked food and have a large selection of books to enjoy."

"Sounds like the perfect place for a solo date," Ella laughs, and thinking about it, she's not wrong. "But that sounds nice; I'd enjoy that."

5

ELLA

I wake up to the sound of banging on my front door. I'm instantly on edge, memories of my life in York seeming to invade my dreams more often now that I've stopped using alcohol to get me to sleep. I look at the clock on my bedside drawers - 1 pm, shit. How have I managed to sleep in so late? I force myself to get out of bed and grab my dressing gown, putting it on quickly.

I take a quick look out of the curtain to see who's visiting me without notice and see my landlord leaning against the entrance way sporting a friendly smile. Though I wish I could bypass the pleasantries, I really do appreciate him letting me move here at such short notice, so I open the front door and invite him in.

"Ah, Ella, we meet in person at last," he says, stepping into the small living room. He's a short, rotund man with greying hair and a walrus moustache and looks exactly like the photo I saw on the listing site. Well, minus the red tie and professional suit, anyway.

"Yes, thank you so much, Mr Briars," I reply politely. "The cottage is absolutely gorgeous, and it's perfect for what I need."

"Glad you like it," he replies in a kind voice. "Me and the wife lived here once, you know. When our son was little. We used to love sitting outside in the garden, listening to the sounds of the sea outside. There's nothing better for clearing your head."

I smile and nod. "That sounds like exactly what I need."

"I'll get my son to bring you some garden furniture over the next time he heads down this way. I meant to do it before we accepted rentals for this year, but I didn't expect to rent this place out for such a long period. My son thought a six-month rental was a good idea, though - less work for us now that we're getting older. What did you say it was you do for a living?"

I blush, still feeling like somewhat of an impostor despite my bestseller. "I'm an author. Historical romance."

"Ah, lovely location for you then. Lots of history in Whitby. You'll be right at home here; the town is full of inspiration. A nice little writing setup in the back garden, and you'll have words spilling from your fingers."

If only. I've got a long way to go before that's my reality again.

"I do hope so," I say, not wanting to overshare.

"Right you are, lass," he says, passing me a piece of paper. "Well, I'd best leave you to it. The wife will be wondering where I am. If you need anything, my number's here. Just don't go phoning too late in the evening - I'm usually tucked up in bed by nine these days."

I thank him again and walk him back to the front door, watching as he walks down the drive and gets into a rusty, old pickup truck. I wave as he leaves and let myself back inside, closing the door behind me.

I'm eager to give Jess a call today. I need to apologise for leaving and not telling her, and I also want her advice about James. I'd absolutely loved our walk along the beach last night, but I'm a bit unsure about whether I'm ready for more than just friendship right now. I do come with a lot of baggage, after all.

After a quick breakfast and shower, I step into the bedroom, my eyes scanning the unfamiliar surfaces as I look for my smartphone. I remember throwing it into a bedroom drawer when I'd first arrived, and it's still there, hidden under old letters and photographs that I'd shoved in there when I'd first unpacked.

I press the power button and watch as the device springs to life. I try to quell my anxiety, just wanting to get Jess's number, nothing more.

I unlock my phone, staring at the familiar icons on my home screen and the photo I'd saved of me and my mother as my wallpaper. But before I can even think, a series of beeps and vibration alerts fill the air as the notifications start to flood in, one after another. Suddenly, the whole screen is engulfed in a flurry of red and blue dots, obscuring any hope of accessing the app I need. I can't help but glance at some of the emails. They pull me in even though I know I can't take it.

Learn to write Ella. Nobody likes your books.

You can't ignore me all the time. I know where you live, remember?

Enjoy your one-star reviews. They're all you deserve.

Would it have hurt you to do even a little bit of research?

You're so ugly. You know you're a fraud as much as I do.

You don't deserve to be a bestseller. Your writing sucks.

You're going to regret moving.

I will find you.

I sink to the floor, my phone slipping through my fingers. Tears stream down my cheeks, and I can't hold back the hysterical sobs that bubble in my chest. How long has he been watching me? What did I do to deserve this? When did my life become somebody else's sick game?

I slump onto the floor, pressing my hands to the sides of my head, trying to block out the relentless beeps and flashes of the notifications that continue to pound through my phone.

I collapse onto the ground, pressing my hands tightly against my ears to drown out the sound. The loud thumping in my chest intensifies, and I lose control of my breathing. My world is spinning, and before I can even think or try and get myself together, everything goes dark.

I PRY my eyelids apart and squint, trying to make sense of the darkness surrounding me. Perspiration covers my brow, and my heart beats erratically in my chest. I push myself up into a sitting position, my temples pounding with pain. Physically, I'm exhausted. Mentally, I'm drained.

My eyes focus on the one thing in the room that's giving off any light: my smartphone. And then it all comes back to me again. I was foolish for thinking I could ever get away from him, for thinking I could isolate myself and heal. I will never escape him. No matter where I go, he will be there.

I force myself to stand and stumble into the living room, my legs shaking as I walk. I need to find a pen and some paper, write Jess's number down, and then throw my phone back into the bottom of the drawer where it belongs.

But as I turn the corner into the living room, I stop in my tracks. There's a man standing in front of the windows, his head tilted upwards, looking out towards the sea. His hands are shoved deep into the pockets of his jeans.

"You'll regret coming here," he says, not turning his head to look at me.

I feel a chill run down the length of my spine, and my next breath catches in my throat. "I'm sorry... who are you?" I ask, trying to find the strength that I know must be inside me somewhere.

"I told you I'd find you," he says.

I rush to the front door, making sure it's locked and then pull all the windows tightly shut, covering them with curtains.

I'm not safe.

I rush to the old house phone that's hanging on the wall and hastily dial Jess's number, hoping she answers quickly. The phone rings and rings, and I beg Jess with all my energy to pick up.

"Hello?"

"Oh, thank god," I reply as I hear the soothing sound of my best friend's voice. "Jess, it's me, I, I need to talk to you. I'm sorry I..."

"Ella? Where have you been? I've been calling you and calling you. You're not at your flat. You've been quiet on Facebook."

"I know," I say, not having the time to explain all this now. This was not the way I had expected this call to go.

"Ella, what's going on?" Jess's voice is soft but firm, and I know she needs answers. "Is it him? What's happened?"

I start to cry, emotions overwhelming me. I wish Jess was here with me. I need a friend so much right now.

"Ella?"

"I left my flat and came to Whitby," I say through muffled sobs. "I thought it would help, but he's found me. I don't know how, but he's here."

"What do you mean he's there? He's emailing again?"

I try hard to hold it together. I have to let Jess know what's going on. I need her.

"Not just emailing. I think he's here in person. There was a man. At the window. He emailed saying I'd regret moving, and then he was here."

"Ella, you need to get off the phone with me and call the police. Do you hear me?"

"I can't," I reply, sobs caught in my throat. "They didn't listen to me last time, did they? They said there was nothing they could do. And it's dark. I didn't even get to see his face. He stood with his back to me. Said what he had to say and left."

"Are you safe right now?" Jess asks, and I can hear the concern in her voice.

"I think so. It seemed like he wanted to frighten me, that's all. He didn't try to force entry or get to me." That thought didn't exactly help me relax, but I couldn't bear to think about the alternative.

"Ok, I want your address; I'm coming over. When I get there, we can decide what we're going to do. But you're not alone in this, Ella. I won't let you deal with this on your own."

My chest relaxes slightly as I give Jess my address. "Maybe I was stupid to have come here in the first place. At least in the city, I knew people, had people who would protect me."

"Just give me an hour to pack some belongings, and I'll be on my way, ok?"

I glance up at the clock, seeing the second hand ticking rapidly around its face. It's a quarter to six.

"Oh no," I say, suddenly remembering James and the book cafe.

"What is it?" Ella asks, worry still evident in her voice.

"I'm supposed to be meeting someone tonight at a cafe in town. I didn't take his number, so I don't know how I'm going to phone and cancel."

"Is it far?" Ella asks me.

"No, just a short drive."

"Ok, change of plan. Can you trust this man you're meeting?"

"I don't know. I mean, he seems nice, but I don't even know his last name."

"Right, I'm going to hope that's a yes. Let me find you a taxi number. You're going to call a taxi and get the driver to pick you up from your cottage, ok? No driving on your own or walking down to the street to get one either."

"There's no chance of that here," I whisper.

"I'll meet you at this cafe and drive you back home. Then we can talk and sort this mess out."

"Jess, I really don't think I can go and be social right now," I say, wiping tears from my cheek. "I look dreadful, I can hardly talk properly, I'm not in any fit state to..."

"Being with somebody else will keep you safe, Ella. And right now, I need to know that you are. It's going to take me a couple of hours to get to you at least, so if you don't want to do this for yourself, do it for me. Whatever you do, don't leave the house until the taxi has pulled up outside, and do not leave the cafe until you're with me. Understood?"

"Understood," I confirm, truly appreciating the efforts that my best friend is willing to go to. "Thanks, Jess. I'll see you in a few hours. It's the book cafe - I don't know the name of the place."

"I know where it is. Stay safe," she replies before hanging up the phone.

～

I STARE BLANKLY at my wardrobe, dreading the evening I'm about to have with James. He was nice enough last night, but making small talk with someone I hardly know is going to be difficult when I can't focus enough to think straight. Why can nothing ever go right in my life?

I reluctantly pull on a clean pair of jeans and an oversized grey jumper, embracing the comfort it brings me as it hugs me close. Not having the energy to do much with my makeup, I wash my face and do the bare minimum before tying my hair in a quick bun. I'm sure the kids would say I'm "effortlessly chic", but I feel anything but.

I glance into the mirror, my reflection staring back at me, revealing a person who's trying to hold themselves together for just one more night. I'd done a good job of masking the nightmare I was living on our beach walk last night, but I think I'll struggle to do it again.

6

JAMES

I stand outside the small bookshop cafe, nervous energy running through my veins. It's a long time since I've felt like this about a woman I've only just met. In fact, I can only remember feeling this way once before in my life, and she'd been the perfect match for me until she left for uni. She'd promised to return after completing her degree, but I don't think I ever really expected her to. Three years away from a small town can change a person.

I squint down at my threadbare watch and give it an impatient tap to make sure it's still working. Ella's fifteen minutes late, and I can't help but wonder if I'm being a fool, standing outside a cafe in the cold night air, waiting for a girl who's clearly too good for me.

With a heavy sigh, I press my face against the fogged-up window and peer inside. The dimmed lighting and soft jazz on the stereo give the place a cosy, inviting vibe, and I'm aching to go in. I rub my arms to fight off the chill and wrap my scarf tighter around my neck. I'm not far off fully shivering and am close to calling it a night and heading home when I see a taxi slowly manoeuvring its way down the street.

I crane my head to try and see through the tinted glass of the taxi, and when it eventually pulls into the spot outside the cafe, I stand up straight and adjust my coat in a pathetic attempt to try and not look as cold as I feel. Relief washes over me as she steps out of the back, handing the driver a fiver through his window. She's not stood me up. Thank the lord!

"Ella," I shout, walking over to her. I can't help but sound enthusiastic. I'm genuinely excited about getting to spend some more time with her.

Ella's cheeks look flushed, and her mouth curves into a timid smile as she meets my gaze. I gesture to the door of the cafe, and she follows me inside. Taking her coat, I lead her to a small table close to the window, pulling out a chair for her. I can feel her gaze on me as I stand behind her chair, and I give her an encouraging smile before taking a step back and taking a seat opposite her.

"I'm sorry I'm late," Ella says as soon as we're both sitting down. "I had a bit of a wait for a taxi, and I didn't have your number to let you know. I hope you weren't waiting long."

My gaze lingers on her as the clatter of cups and plates from the coffee shop echoes through the air. She's wearing a soft, oversized jumper, the deep charcoal hue making her appear even smaller than she is, and her hair is pulled back in a low bun that only accentuates her delicate features. Our eyes meet, and there's a pause, a moment of recognition between us. She nervously bites her lip, and I want nothing more than to take her into my arms.

"No, not long," I reply, reassuring her. "I was only slightly worried you'd changed your mind."

I wink, and Ella considers me for a moment, her eyes inspecting my face. She clasps her hands together and blushes. "You're not what I expected," she says slowly as if trying to figure something out.

"What did you expect?" I ask.

She stills, seeming to ponder the question.

"I wasn't sure," she finally responds. "When you first approached me yesterday afternoon, I wasn't expecting to find out that the guy I'd seen drinking a caramel latte was one, a fisherman, two, romantic and three, a fan of books. And now here I am. Enjoying a second evening out with someone who's full of surprises."

I laugh. "I know, I'm a bit of an odd one."

"Odd in a good way," she says, smiling.

The conversation dies away, and I look over to one of the waitresses, alerting her that we're ready for coffee. As we wait, a gruff-looking man dressed in three layers of pea coats shuffles over to the counter, empty cup in hand.

"If you're still serving coffee, I'd like one. Please," he says to the woman, an exaggeration placed on the word *please*. I wonder what's got his goat. He looks at Ella and me and frowns disapprovingly.

Before I can joke about it, I feel the air around us growing heavy and tense and sense Ella's body language stiffening. Something isn't right here.

"Do you know that man?" I ask, shifting my chair closer to hers. She ignores me, neither responding nor looking up.

I hear a loud cough, and the man walks past us, hot coffee in hand. I watch as he steps out into the night air, his eyes darting to us one last time before he leaves.

With a slight shake of her head, Ella lets out a breath that seems to have been held for far too long. I can tell she's uncomfortable.

"Ella? What is it?" I ask, more pointedly this time.

"No, I don't know him," she replies.

I want to press her, find out what's bothering her, but the waitress returns to take our order.

"Who was that man?" I ask again after she's left. "Why did he make you feel so uneasy?"

Ella rubs the back of her hand across her forehead, and I notice she seems on edge like she's unsure how much to share with me. Maybe I should have just dropped it.

"I don't know," she mumbles quietly. Her eyes drop down to the table. "I just get that feeling everybody gets, I guess, the one where you're being watched. I felt it in the market a couple of days ago too. It just makes me uncomfortable."

I can tell she's not telling me the whole story, but I decide to leave it, not wanting to push her.

Ella looks up at me and smiles, breaking the momentary tension between us. "Were you thinking of ordering any food?" she asks, changing the subject.

I look at the menu the waitress left on the table for us, scanning the long list of soups, sandwiches, and burgers, each one more tempting than the last. But it's the lobster club that catches my eye. I'm a sucker for lobster, bacon, and ripe tomatoes, all nestled between slices of toasted bread.

"The lobster club," I reply casually, my mouth watering at the thought. "It's delicious, and the lobster is as fresh as it comes."

Ella smiles, and the awkwardness between us is broken. I can see her start to visibly relax again, and I let out a breath I didn't realise I'd been holding.

"A lobster club it is, then," she says brightly. "I'll have the same." Nodding to herself, she gets up and heads over to the counter to place our order.

When she returns, we chat about all kinds of things - our childhoods, love of books, hopes for the future, and those things that make us who we are. It feels relaxed now, and I feel the knot of tension from earlier in the evening loosen a bit. I'm blown away by the fact that she's a published author, and make a mental note to buy a copy of her book when I get home.

After a delicious meal, we settle into getting to know each other some more, the weird man from earlier in the evening soon forgotten. I'm enjoying every minute of this evening with Ella, even as it grows late. I've got to be up early in the morning for another day on the boat, but I'm in no rush for this date to end. Paul will kill me, but it's 100% worth it.

As I listen to Ella recount stories about various friends, I laugh, and she smiles shyly, unaware of just how adorable she looks.

I'm laughing at her latest story when I hear the tinkling of the doorbell. I look up, distracted, and see a woman walk inside, a gust of cool air following her. She's wearing a long black wool coat, which hangs just above her knees, and her gentle face has a look of concern deeply etched onto it. I watch as she looks around the cafe anxiously, her eyes finally settling on Ella.

"Jess," Ella cries, and before I know what's happening, the woman rushes over to our table and wraps Ella into a tight hug.

"Oh, I'm so glad the cafe is still open. I was driving so fast over here that I thought I'd get pulled over. And then I had to find a parking space and wait for the bridge to come down..."

"There's a car park a two-minute walk away," I laugh, forcing myself into their conversation. "I'm James, by the way."

I watch as the woman looks me up and down, and I can't say I don't feel a little hurt by Ella inviting someone else on our date. Ok, it's not a date, but still. Had she texted her and begged her to come after the awkward start to our night? She could have told her she wasn't needed. I'd thought things had been going better.

"Hey, don't I know you?" the woman replies, taking off her right glove and shaking my hand.

"Sorry, James," Ella interjects. "Jess is my best friend, and I'd asked her to come over way before I got here. She said she'd pick me up from the cafe to save me the cost of a taxi home. It wasn't one of those "text me if you need a get out" things. I promise she would not have driven over two hours to reach me for that."

"I can confirm," Jess laughs. "What did you say your last name was again?"

"I didn't," I say. "But it's Clarke."

"Oh. My. God. James Clarke! I totally do know you. You went to Peafield Academy, didn't you? Remember a Jessica Beaver?"

"How could I forget a name like that?" I laugh.

"What a small world, eh? What're the chances of the best-looking guy at that place hooking up with my best friend?"

"Jess, we didn't-" Ella chimes in, and I can't help but feel slightly hurt.

"I'd better be off soon anyway," I say, not wanting to intrude on their reunion any longer. "Early morning on the boat. It was lovely seeing you again tonight, Ella, and I'd love to do it again sometime".

I steel myself, not wanting to get my hopes up too high.

Ella looks away from Jess and takes my hand. "I'd love that," she says. "I don't have a smartphone at the moment for reasons I can't go into right now, but if you give me your number, I can call you."

Ah, the classic give me your number line.

I grab a pen and write my number on the back of one of the unused coasters sitting on the table. I hand it to Ella, who takes it from me.

She places it into her pocket, and before I know what's happening, she's kissed me on the cheek goodbye. It's quick, innocent and leaves me wanting more.

"It was nice seeing you again too, Jess," I say politely, not quite able to meet her eyes. We weren't exactly friends when we were kids, and I was well aware of all the stories about her—the reasons why she'd left town.

I get up and walk over to pay for the sandwiches and coffee, the women's voices starting up again the second my back is turned.

My hand falters as I reach into my pocket to grab my wallet. In the few seconds that follow, I try to get my head around everything that happened this evening. I finally manage to pull out some notes and hand them to the barista.

"Keep the change," I say with a heavy smile, and I turn, ready to leave this strange but wonderful girl behind me.

"James!" Ella calls, and I spin around as I hear her stand up. "I meant it, you know? I really do want to see you again."

7

ELLA

I t's late by the time I get back to my cottage with Jess beside me, and the last thing I want to do is go through everything right now. Jess is in agreement that a good night's sleep will help, and I promise to explain everything in the morning. I make up the spare bed for her with some sheets the landlord had left in the airing cupboard, triple-check that all the doors and windows are locked and say goodnight.

However, once I get into bed, I struggle to clear my mind. So much has happened today that I have so many thoughts rushing through my brain. From the unexpected meeting with my landlord to the weird man at my house, the date with James, the second weird man at the coffee shop, and then Jess turning up, and James' reaction to her. I wish I could start writing again just to get some of my thoughts out of my head.

The wind howls loudly around the cottage, and at some point in the night, rain starts to fall heavily. I pull my dressing gown on and walk to one of the windows overlooking the rocky coastline, surprised to see lightning lighting up the sky. Odd for March, but nothing surprises me much anymore.

I quietly move around in the kitchen, trying not to wake Jess, and make myself a cup of herbal tea, taking it back to bed with me. I snuggle up in my covers and sip it slowly as I try to make sense of everything going on.

I must fall asleep at some point as I awake to the smell of breakfast cooking and pots and pans bashing around in the kitchen.

I drag myself out of bed and walk into the living room.

"Morning stranger," I didn't think you were ever going to get up, Jess laughs. "If I didn't know better, I'd have thought you'd gone on a bender last night and didn't get home until closing time."

I smile and take the mug of hot tea Jess passes me.

"I nipped out this morning and bought some fresh bread and bacon, so I'm just making us some sarnies. I'll be in shortly. You just put your feet up, and I'll bring them straight through."

It's so lovely to have my best friend here looking after me. I really will have to make sure to tell her how much I appreciate her.

A few minutes later, Jess walks over to me, two plates in one hand and her own mug of tea in the other. I take a plate from her and sink my teeth into a delicious bacon sandwich. It's so good!

"You weren't joking when you said you'd been out this morning," I say, half wondering what time it is. "I hope you realise there's no way I'll be letting you leave if you make me breakfast this good!"

Jess smiles and sits down in an armchair opposite me. "I told my boss I need a week off. I didn't give her any specifics, but if I'm needed for longer, don't you worry; I'll work something out."

"I'm sorry, Jess," I say, not quite sure where to start. I finish my bite and take a drink before I begin to speak. "I thought I was doing the right thing when I came here. I wanted not to have to rely on you as much as I was starting to, and I needed to sort my life out. I planned to phone you yesterday to tell you where I was and why I'd moved. I just didn't expect to have to call you as freaked out as I was".

As I recount what happened yesterday, I'm suddenly fearful for my safety again. I quickly jump up to check that Jess locked the door when she returned this morning.

"I locked it," she says, easing my mind. "And I locked you in when I left, too. I wouldn't put you at risk."

I smile and sit back down.

Between bites of bacony goodness, I tell Jess everything that's happened since I got here. I mention the emails, the ensuing panic attack, the man who stood by the window and said he'd found me, the man in the coffee shop, and I also tell her about James. Poor sweet James, who probably feels like he's wasted a night of his life thanks to me and how I acted.

When I'm done talking, I have tears running down my face. Jess takes my hands in hers and wipes my tears away.

"Ella, listen to me." Jess has her stern voice on. I'm used to the stern voice. It usually means I'm about to do precisely what she says. And to be honest, I think that's what I need right now. "You need to phone the police."

"I can't Jess. I've already tried, and you saw what happened. They told me it was just part of being in the public eye, and they made it very clear they weren't a security service for part-time authors. I'm not budging on this. It's me who needs to find a way to sort this mess out. The police can't help me."

Jess considers me for a moment, and I can tell she's trying to find the right words.

"OK," she says, "I still think we are going to need to speak to the police, especially if this man shows up at the house again. But in the meantime, we can come up with a plan together. I'll go out after breakfast and get you a new phone and a new phone number so at least you can contact the people you need to without having to read his messages every time you look at your phone."

"I've been thinking about doing that, too," I tell her. It might only be a temporary solution, but if I can set up a new phone that has the details of my close friends and my publisher on it, at least people will still be able to contact me, and I won't have to deal with the anxiety of my old phone.

"If you're ok with it, I'll also take a look at your old phone and see if anyone has been trying to get in touch with you that's important and that you need to speak to. If I do it, you won't be forced to look at the emails - or any other type of notification - that could upset you."

I take a deep breath and consider her words. "Thank you," I say, knowing she's speaking sense.

"Also, don't worry about James," she reassures me. "From what I remember of him at school, he's a great guy, and he won't be thinking poorly of you just because of this. If anything, you've probably spiced his life up a little bit. Very little fun happens in Whitby out of season - trust me, it's one of the main reasons I moved."

When Jess says that, I feel a little better. I hadn't considered developing a romantic relationship with James when he'd first asked me out. Still, his smile was infectious last night, and I appreciated how protective he was of me despite not really knowing me. Plus, we had so many similar interests, we really could have talked for hours.

If the timing had been right, and I hadn't moved here due to the circumstances I had, maybe I'd have been a lot keener and not been such a crappy date.

I make a point to head down to the harbour on Monday, thank him for the date, and suggest meeting again in person. I owe him a bit of an explanation. Maybe not the whole stalker explanation - that would scare anyone straight off - but enough for him to understand what's going on.

"We need to keep you safe, Ella. We'll sort the rest out together," Jess says, snapping me out of my thoughts.

"Thank you," I say to her again. I suddenly feel a hundred times better just knowing that she's here with me. I also feel a little embarrassed that it has taken all of this to make me realise how much of a friend she really is. I shouldn't have shut her out when I moved here. It was a terrible thing to do to her.

A COUPLE OF HOURS LATER, Jess is back with a brand-new phone for me and a Pay as You Go sim card. I start setting it up while Jess goes through my old phone, reviewing old texts and monitoring how many calls and messages I've missed over the last few days.

Aside from all the messages and calls from Jess herself, the only other person of any importance who's tried to contact me is my publisher, Jane. I'm supposed to be meeting up with her next week with the next few chapters of my new book, and as I haven't been able to write a thing since the abuse and my drinking got out of hand, I'm dreading it.

"You can do it," Jess reassures me, writing my publisher's email address and phone number down for me.

I set up a new Gmail account on my new phone and write an email to Jane, explaining why I'm using a new address and why I haven't responded to any calls. I explain that it's been hard for me to write and that I'd love to arrange a Skype or Zoom call with her next week instead of an in-person meeting, which is pretty difficult at the moment.

My stomach churns as I hit send on the email. My publisher always responds quickly, one of the benefits of working with a small press, I guess, but the seconds between the "send" and the response seem to drag on. Luckily, around ten minutes later, my phone pings to let me know she's replied.

I look at Jess with a grin as I read her the email.

"By the sounds of this," Jess says, "she seems to care more about you as a human being than a writer."

"She's probably regretting giving me an advance," I say, only half joking. "I bet she won't do that again in a hurry."

It's hard to explain, but somehow just letting Jane know what I've been dealing with has lightened the load a little bit. It doesn't justify me not doing the work I'd agreed to, but I feel better knowing I'm not the only one dealing with this secret right now.

A few minutes later, Jess places my old phone back down on the coffee table.

"I had no idea you were dealing with so much," she says to me, her brow furrowing. "When you said things were bad, I expected a negative review and a couple of emails. What I've just seen is - I'm sorry, there's no other word for it - insane!"

"Has he sent any more since yesterday?" I ask, half wanting to know whether the man who stood outside my window yesterday was him and half wanting to live in ignorance.

"No," Jess replies. "The last one was sent yesterday at 11.12 am. If you don't mind, I'll check your phone daily. I will filter everything he sends into a separate folder in case we need it in the future. I know you said you don't trust the police to help right now, but with this amount of evidence, I think they will take you seriously."

My shoulders slump in relief momentarily, only for anxiety to re-enter my stomach. Has he stopped emailing because he can just observe me now? I feel a shudder of fear run through me at the thought. The thought of him watching me without my knowledge is terrifying.

8

JAMES

I pull on a pair of freshly washed jeans and grab my favourite black t-shirt from its perch on my bedpost before pulling it over my head. A cartoon fish wearing a top hat smiles up at me from the shirt - it usually makes me chuckle every time I look at it, but not tonight. I spray on a quick spritz of aftershave and run a comb through my hair. A quick look in the mirror, and I'm all set. It's Sunday night, which means a night at the Stag's Head with Paul and Beth for the local quiz.

I'd spent much of the weekend hoping that Ella would call. She's been in my thoughts a lot the past two days, and I would have loved for her to join us, even just as a friend. But it doesn't look like it's meant to be. I couldn't say I wasn't disappointed, but I guess I understood. She had her best friend here with her now. She didn't need me or anybody else.

I grab my house keys and walk the short distance to the pub. The clocks had gone forward an hour the night before, so it feels earlier than it actually is, and I find myself walking faster than usual. I meander around the harbour where I meet Paul every morning for work and continue up the main road, finally spotting the distinctive, maroon-coloured sign of the pub in the distance.

I push open the door to the pub and am greeted by a crowd of shouting and cheering locals, some already sporting the signs of too much beer. Jeff and Sheila, who work behind the bar, grin at me as I walk up to them to order a pint of beer.

"Alright James, all ready for the quiz tonight?" Jeff asks me as he pours my beer.

"Yeah, looking forward to it," I reply as I scan the room, looking for Paul and Beth. I spot Beth sitting at a small table near the window and wave. Paul is standing a couple of tables away, speaking to some of the other guys who work on the fishing boats with us. I smile and nod as one of them catches my eye.

Seconds later, a loud voice, amplified by a microphone, booms over all the others, calling for order and for the quiz to start. I thank Jeff for my pint and hand over some coins before carrying it over to the little table Beth has saved for us near the window.

"Hey, how are you?" asks Beth as I pull up a seat.

"I'm good," I say, pulling a pen and quiz sheet towards me and gazing absent-mindedly out the window. I watch as a fishing trawler gets loaded with crates stacked up on the quay, presumably ready for tomorrow.

"You don't look ok mate. What's up?" she asks, pulling my mind back to the pub.

I watch as Paul says his farewells to the other fishermen and comes to join us. I might as well tell them about Ella at the same time. It's not like it's something I want to repeat.

"Meh, I'm a bit grumpy because Ella hasn't called me, I guess."

"Oh man, that sucks," says Paul as he sits down with his pint. "And I thought it had gone well too. At least, you didn't text me to call you saying my house was on fire," he laughed.

"What?" Beth asked, smirking. "You're not still using that old line, are you?"

I watch as Paul takes a sip of his beer and laughs louder, and I can't help rolling my eyes. It wasn't funny the first time he suggested using that as a get-out clause.

"Well, I mean, we had a good time, and the evening passed way too quickly. Honestly, I could have chatted to her all night once we'd got the awkward pleasantries out of the way. That doesn't mean it's meant to lead anywhere,e but it would have been nice for her to call, wouldn't it? I guess the fact she hasn't says it all."

"I wouldn't read too much into it just yet," Beth says kindly. "Paul said you went out a couple of times, and if you had as good a night as you said, I'm sure you'll see her again."

I shrug and take a sip of my beer.

"It's only been a couple of days. Can't you phone her?"

"Nope. She said she doesn't have a mobile," I reply.

"Everybody take your seats. The quiz is about to begin," Graham, the quiz master, calls out, interrupting our conversation.

"Who doesn't have a phone?" Beth whispers to me, and all I can do is shrug. I had thought it odd at the time but didn't want to pry to find out it was code for *just not interested now that my friend is here.*

I watch Graham take the microphone and settle everyone down for a second time. Usually, I like the concept of the quiz. It's a good way to meet people, have a bit of friendly banter, if not a bit of competition, and it's a good reason to leave the house over the winter months, but I'm really not feeling it today.

Paul and Beth chatter animatedly as I sit lost in my thoughts. If I'm honest with myself, I'm not sure why I even came tonight. I put a brave face on it, but I'm sick of being the third wheel in their relationship. I'm sure Beth gets sick of me tagging along all the time.

"Question 1," Graham speaks into the microphone, his voice echoing around the pub. "How many ghosts chase Pac-Man at the start of each game?"

Easy. I quickly scribble down the answer - 4 - not even waiting for Paul or Beth to chime in.

"Question 2: Which planet has the most moons?"

I turn my gaze from the quiz sheet to the bar where two women dressed in scantily clad outfits are frantically competing to answer the quiz master's latest question, their shouts nearly drowning out the cheer of the rowdy group in football shirts singing off-key. A few tables away, an elderly couple in matching tweed jackets shoots the revellers' daggers from beneath the brims of their woolly hats, and a man on his own sits nursing a pint while looking utterly forlorn.

"Question 5: What were the names of Henry VIII's wives?"

Beth yanks the quiz sheet out of my hands and begins scribbling down the answers to the questions I've missed. I'm quickly losing interest; my eyelids feel heavy, and I'm making slow progress on my beer. I put my head in my hands, really not feeling too great, and wonder whether I can get away with leaving early.

Just then, the uncomfortable feeling in my side returns, and I gasp sharply.

"James, what is it?" Beth asks me, her face etched with worry. I feel a white-hot wave of pain lance through my abdomen, and I push my hand into it, unable to speak. It takes a few seconds, but the pain gradually ebbs, and once I'm able, I stand up and stumble over to the men's toilets, feeling Beth's gaze on me as I go.

I push open the door to one of the small cubicles, the hinges creaking with age, and ease myself into a sitting position, locking the door behind me. My stomach feels bloated, and for once, I know it's not down to me drinking too much. I've not even had half a pint since I arrived.

"Not again," I mutter to myself. This is the third time this week, and I'm starting to think Paul is right - I need to get myself to the doctor. I push my fingers into my side again as if I can somehow massage the pain away. It's better than nothing, and right now, it's all I can do.

I'm just about to get up when I hear the door to the men's open, and I still, not wanting anyone from work to see me like this.

"Are you alright in there?" a voice shouts through the door. It's Beth. God, why did she have to come and check on me?

"Fine," I reply, my voice quite curt. "I'll be back out in a minute."

"Okay," she shouts in reply. "Here if you need me."

I force myself to stand, the pain in my abdomen still there yet not as bad as it had been a few minutes before. I unlock the cubicle door and walk over to the sinks, turning both taps to the coldest setting and splashing water on my face. The icy water stings as it courses down my cheeks, but I welcome the pain. *What is wrong with you man?*

I shuffle over to the urinals and take a leak as quietly as I'm able, not wanting Beth to hear. Knowing her, she won't have returned to the table, and I don't want her to listen in on me.

"You okay out there?" she shouts again. *Knew it.*

I sigh heavily, making sure my voice is loud enough for her to hear, "Yeah...I'm f -". I'm cut off by another wave of pain that makes me double over.

"Are you okay?" Beth calls again, impatient this time. "James? Hello? Is something wrong?" Her voice starts panicking.

I hear footsteps outside the door, and seconds later, Paul has joined me. I rush to zip myself up, not wanting him to see me like this, but the pain is overwhelming.

"Mate, what's going on?" Paul asks me, his voice laced with concern.

I gasp. "I have no idea, man. I'm in agony."

"Crap, mate, what do you need?" he asks me, helping me to stand up.

I hammer at my stomach with my fist. "Just take it easy, James," Paul advises between my stifled groans of pain.

Eventually, the pain relents and my breathing returns to normal. I shake my head at Paul. "I've no idea; my side is killing me, though."

Paul nods at me and gives me a weak smile. "You sure you don't want to get yourself checked out? It might be appendicitis."

"Yeah," I reply. "I'm starting to think that maybe I should."

"Good," says Paul, patting my shoulder and leading me out of the bathroom. "What do you think?" he asks Beth, who's still standing outside the door, craning her neck to look inside, no doubt worried about me. "He might have appendicitis?"

She frowns. "Do you want to go to the hospital? I can take you there if you'd rather not drive."

I shake my head. "Thanks for the offer, but no thanks. I'll go in the morning and get it checked out."

"But what if it's serious?" she asks me, her face pleading.

"I don't think it's appendicitis," I say, trying to put a brave face on it. "If it was, my appendix would have burst by now. It's probably something minor. I'll phone the doctor in the morning."

"Yeah, take the day off work, mate," Paul tells me. "You can't come in like that. Better to get yourself sorted, don't you think?"

I nod and smile at Beth, gently touching her shoulder. "I'll be alright, I promise. Probably going to head off home now, though. I can't stomach any more to drink tonight."

Beth gives me a strange look and nods her head slowly. "If you're sure."

"I am. Sorry for ruining the evening."

Paul gives me a hug. "We'll catch up later, yeah?"

"Of course."

I walk out of the pub, stepping out onto the cobbled street. The smell of fish and chips lingers in the air, but for once, I'm not hungry. I take a moment to watch the sun dip low in the sky, painting the horizon with a fiery orange colour. Whitby is stunning at night, but my heavy feeling remains.

My thoughts turn to Ella and why she hasn't called, and I can't help but feel frustrated with both that and the repeated abdominal pains I keep experiencing. It's rare for me to take a day off work, and I hate doing it to Paul. I feel like I'm a bit of a waste of space all around at the moment.

I shake my head, chastising myself for my dark musings. I'm making something out of nothing. If Ella's interested, she will call me, and Dr Todd will likely have a simple explanation for my stomach and flu issues. I try not to worry as I take a slow walk home.

9

ELLA

The sun shines through the bedroom curtains early Monday morning, filling the room with a warm glow. As I roll over, I hear the sound of the coffee maker humming in the kitchen, and the smell of freshly brewed coffee wafts into the room. I smile, really glad that Jess is still here for a couple more days before she has to return to York for work.

She's been here all weekend, and although she says she'll stay as long as I need, I don't want to put her in an awkward position. The accounting firm she works for is small, and I'm sure they're missing her already. I make a mental note to reach out to her boss and thank them for allowing her to take some time off last minute. It's not Jess's fault that her best friend is a mess.

I throw a dressing gown on over my pyjamas and walk the few steps into the living room, where Jess is waiting for me, a mug of warm coffee in hand.

"So, what's the plan for today," she asks me.

"Well," I say, pouring myself a coffee and sitting down. "I thought we could maybe walk around Whitby a bit today. We could visit the abbey, do a bit of shopping on Church Street, and take a stroll down by the harbour."

"Is this a fun tourist day out, or are you planning on staying here long term?" Jess asks me, raising her eyebrows.

"I'm not sure," I say honestly. "I've got this cottage until October, and I'm not in any rush to decide where I live after that. I can't imagine any locations that are more inspiring for writing, and Jane didn't seem to have an issue with me moving, so if I can just find a way to deal with that man-"

Jess looks at me, concern etched on her face again.

"I've been thinking about that," she says, placing her mug on the coffee table in front of her. "Do you think your landlord might be willing to install some security features up here for you? I mean, I know it's advertised as an isolated cottage in the middle of nowhere, but in your situation, I don't think that's necessarily a good thing."

"I can ask him," I say, agreeing.

"I mean, I don't know if he'd be willing to go the whole hog and install security cameras, but a couple of motion sensor lights and a Ring doorbell would improve your safety. You'd be notified of any movement outside, and your doorbell would video-record anyone who even thinks of coming close to the door. I hope that dung beetle has returned to the mud heap he crawled out of, but if not, you'd think it would be a good deterrent, and it will also give you more evidence should you decide to go to the police at some point."

"Yeah," I say, biting my lip. "That would scare him off, one way or the other."

Jess takes a tentative sip of her coffee, the steam curling towards her face as she locks her gaze on mine. She places her hand lightly on my arm, the heat from her touch warming my skin. Her eyes light up as she discusses the plan. If Mr Briars agrees, I'd be happy to foot the bill, and it would certainly make me feel safer.

"I'll call him now."

I walk into the kitchen and pick up the piece of paper containing Mr Briars' phone number. I store him as a contact in my new phone, press 'call' and wait for it to connect.

"Hello?"

"Oh, hi, Mr Briars. It's Ella. The girl renting your cottage."

"Oh, hello, Ella. I didn't notice your number there for a second. Got a new phone, have you?"

"Yes. My old one broke," I reply, not wanting to give him many specifics about my situation.

It doesn't take long to make my request about the security features, and luckily, he immediately agrees. "It's something else I've been planning to do for a while," he tells me, and I'm also not the first guest who's suggested it, so that's both good and a little unnerving. I thank him for his kindness and return to Jess, my face beaming.

"He agreed then?" she asks me, relief flooding her features.

"Yep, said he'll sort it out this week for me."

"Did you explain why?" Jess asks, more out of curiosity.

"I gave him a few details," I reply. "I mentioned the man I saw at the window last week, and he didn't seem overly shocked."

"That's reassuring," Jess laughs. "Almost sounds like it could be a normal thing to happen around here."

I smile. "I mean, it's not great, is it? But if it's happened before, there's a chance it's not the same man who keeps emailing me."

"True," Jess agrees. "Well, this all sounds positive, and your land-lord sounds great. It's making me feel better about leaving you here on your own."

"I'll be fine," I promise her. I can still feel the tension in my muscles, but I'm sure things will be better once I've got some safety precautions in place. Plus, I have a new phone now, and I've made a friend in James, so I have people close if I need them. Taking it easy for a little while is still my plan of action for now, but with any luck, I'll be able to heal a bit and start writing again. I already feel better having a break from the notifications of my old life.

AFTER FINISHING our coffees and getting dressed, I drive Jess into town and park up near the abbey. The sky has turned overcast, and the pale sunlight that warmed me earlier has disappeared. Instead, a gloomy film hangs over the town, shrouding the buildings and turning the ground grey. The wind has picked up too, and I watch people scurrying down on the beach below, trying to shelter from it.

Still, bad weather isn't a problem - in fact, there's nothing I like more at times - and it means there won't be many people up here, so we can walk around in peace.

We pay for our tickets and walk into Whitby Abbey, marvelling at its size. Despite visiting the town numerous times as a child, I've never actually stepped foot in the abbey, my parents never having the money to spend on attractions. I remember feeling disappointed that we could never explore the building that dominated the town's skyline, and it's pretty cool to be doing it now with Jess.

To our left, a vast wall stretches down the length of the Abbey, built from thick stone and dotted with arches along the way. We walk toward it, observing the details in awe until we reach the entrance, where steps lead into an indoor room with wooden benches positioned around the floor. We take a seat and take in more of the details: statues of saints, some looking down at us, others towering over us from further up in the room.

"This place is almost making me want to write," Jess laughs as she walks around, taking everything in and committing it to memory.

"You should!" I encourage her. "Maybe you'll be the next Bram Stoker."

She gently pushes me, a wide grin plastered on her face, and it's nice to be joking around in the way we used to before everything that was now my life became such a tangled mess. For the briefest of moments, I'm able to ignore my worries and simply enjoy the moment for what it is. It's been so long since I last felt this way.

"Ha, not likely. I'm only good at coming up with ideas for you remember? It would be fun to just up and leave, though, like you did. Imagine how many fun adventures we could have if I didn't have a 9-5."

"Literally the dream," I respond. I drag Jess to the abbey's museum, my excitement increasing as I spot a rare, signed copy of Dracula.

"Signed by the man himself," Jess mouths to me as she reads it, and I can't help but feel inspired. This is actually incredible for a book geek like me. I hope I can channel some of this energy into writing my own novel.

Before I can reply, I notice a movement out of the side of my eye. I turn quickly, but all I can see is shadow.

"What is it?" Jess asks, moving closer to me until our fingers are touching.

"I thought I saw something," I reply, a shiver going through my spine. My eyes struggle to adjust to the dim light, and I can't be sure if it was a passer-by or just my mind playing tricks on me.

"Was it him?" she asks me, her face concerned.

"There's someone in here, I'm sure of it," I speak quietly. I look around once more, but the shadows and dim light of the room give nothing away.

I realise my hand is sweaty and wipe it on my jeans while trying to refill the air in my lungs. Jess grasps my hand and leads me back outside into the open air, which helps lower my panic and steady my breathing. I stand rigid, looking at the door to the museum, but nobody comes out. The abbey is deserted, and I curse myself for letting things get the better of me once again.

"You okay?" Jess asks, her hands wrapped gently around my shoulders to steady me.

"Yeah," I try and nod, but it comes out more of a nervous twitch. "I'm okay."

"Are you sure?" I can hear the worried tone in her voice.

"Yeah, sorry. Honestly, I'm fine. But maybe we should leave, go and look around the shops for a bit?"

"Ella, there's absolutely nothing wrong with being worried or scared," she tells me firmly. "You've been through a really tough time of it lately."

I fall into her arms, letting her hug me tight. I really wish I could snap out of it, but I guess it's not that easy when you've been subjected to the constant abuse I have. I can't help but feel like everyone is out to get me, even if I know in my head that's not true.

"Thank you," I say to her. "For not making me think I'm crazy."

"You're not crazy, Ella," she says.

I let Jess take my hand and walk me out of the abbey. We head down the windy paths and through the hidden alleyways until we reach Church Street. A milkshake shop on the corner stands empty, nobody wanting to enjoy a cold shake when the weather's this bad. We pass independent stores selling everything from bath bombs to homeware, and I look up as I see the book café I visited with James last week.

"Fancy going in there again?" Jess asks me.

"Sure," I reply. "It's warm and cosy, and they make a delicious lobster club."

We sit down at a table in the middle of the room, and Jess heads to the counter to place our orders.

"So, you never did tell me what happened on your date the other night," she says as she sits down across from me.

"It wasn't a date Jess," I say, though I feel a blush creep up my cheeks, totally giving away how I actually feel.

"Ok, but you liked him though, didn't you?" she pries. "You looked like you were having a great time when I turned up."

If I was honest with myself, she was completely right. I did enjoy his company, and I'd completely lost track of time by the time Jess arrived. But I'd also been a peculiar 'date,' and I wouldn't blame James if he wanted nothing to do with me.

I smile at Jess. She could read me like a book; I didn't need to use words.

"So...," she asks. "Are you going to call him?"

"Maybe," I say. "Or maybe we could go for a walk by the harbour and see if I can speak to him in person. His fishing boat should be returning soon."

"You already know his schedule?" Jess laughs, and I can't help but blush again.

"No," I protest. "I just know what time I saw him return the other day and assume it'll be the same today."

"Come on then," she jests. "I'll see if we can take our coffees and clubs to go."

◠

WE MEANDER down the cobblestone path and across the bridge, taking in the architecture and friendly chatter of the locals. Twenty minutes later, we emerge on the other end of town, where the harbour stretches before us. Fishing vessels and sailboats bob in the distance, their masts dipping in and out of view against the glistening grey of the water.

"Can you see his boat?" Jess asks me. She pulls her coat tighter against her, trying to shield herself from the wind.

I squint, straining my eyes to make out the shapes of the boats in the blur of the harbour. Dozens of vessels dance in the choppy water, their decks full of fishermen unloading their catches into crates, loud voices ringing out in the salty air. "I don't think so."

We stroll along the dock, the waves lapping rhythmically against the hulls of the boats. I scan each face, searching for his broad shoulders, my heart quickening with anticipation. But try as I might, I can't pick James out of the throng.

"Maybe he's already been and gone," Jess suggests, and I can't help but feel deflated.

Just as we reach the end of the harbour, I see a man who looks somewhat familiar. It's not James, but it could be his best friend, Paul. There's only one way to find out. I pass my sandwich to Jess and let her know I'll be back in a minute.

"Hi," I say brightly as I approach, having no idea how to approach this stranger and wondering where this sudden burst of confidence is coming from. "Paul, right?"

"Oh yes," he smiles at me before looking at Jess, who is watching us intently. "Do I know you? Don't tell me. You joined us on one of the tourist fishing trips last season?"

He has a thick Yorkshire accent and bushy eyebrows that make him look very kind and welcoming. His cheeks are ruddy, but his eyes are wide and twinkle with warmth as he stares back at me, waiting for an answer.

"No," I laugh. "I'm Ella-"

"Ohhhhhhh, Ella, I have heard a lot about you!" Paul winks. "Ok, I probably shouldn't have said that - don't tell James, will you? He's forever telling me to stop meddling in his love life."

I can't help but laugh again. I can see why they're best friends.

"I won't," I promise. "Is James not working today?"

"No," he answers stoically. "Bad stomach. I suggested he take the day off. I can give him a message for you, though, if you'd like?"

I think about it, but I'm not sure what message I'd like him to pass on. I hadn't planned for this.

"Maybe just tell him I popped by?" I say. "I'm sure I'll see him around."

"Sure thing," Paul replies, picking up another crate and resting it on his shoulder. "It was nice meeting you."

"Likewise," I smile. I wave a quick goodbye and return to Jess, watching the boats as Paul disappears into the crowd.

10

JAMES

I throw my keys down onto the counter and slump down into the sofa, kicking my shoes off in the process. I'd had to wait until nearly 4 pm for my doctor's appointment, and even getting that was like pulling teeth. The slots had already been filled by the time I got through on the phone this morning, and I'd had to pretty much plead with the receptionist for an emergency appointment to get myself seen. It was beyond a joke.

And, rather than feeling assured that everything was fine, I was now more worried than ever. Dr Todd had ruled out appendicitis quickly but insisted on running some blood tests, which he'd sent me for immediately. He'd also scheduled me for a colonoscopy at the Community Hospital in two days' time. My dad had gone through the same thing when I was a baby, my mum not bothering to spare the details when I'd asked about it. I was well aware of how this was going to go.

"Fuck," I scream into the ether. I want to punch something, smash my fists into the wall until I'm exhausted. This isn't me, it isn't who I am, but I'm not ready for this to be the end. And I know, within a couple of days, I'll be preparing for that fact.

I turn the TV on and try to find something to watch, to take my mind off these intruding thoughts, but it's no good. I flip through channel after channel until I turn it off and throw the remote at the wall in a rage. I need to do something productive, not just sit here and wait to be told the inevitable.

I pace around my tiny flat, pushing my fingers through my hair with nervous energy, and stop in front of a framed picture of my parents. It had been taken on Whitby beach not long before I was born, my mother's pregnancy clear. Had they known about my dad's death sentence when this photo was taken? They look so happy together. I guess that's how you feel when you're madly in love and are just a few short weeks away from bringing a baby into the world.

My thoughts are interrupted by the sudden, jarring sound of my phone blaring from the coffee table in front of me. I jump towards it, my heart pounding in my chest. Could this be Ella? I glance at the screen and see Paul's name glaring back at me in big, bold letters. I sigh and swipe my finger to accept the call.

"Now then, pal," the sound of my best friend's voice fills my ears. "Feeling any better?"

I let out a sigh and sink back down into the sofa. "Not in the slightest, mate," I reply. "I'm gonna need to take tomorrow and the day after off work too. Todd's sending me to the hospital for some tests, and I've got to take some medication to empty my stomach before-hand. Don't think you'd be too impressed dealing with me crapping my pants at sea."

"Oh shit, mate, that doesn't sound too good. Though I bet you he's just covering all bases and doesn't want to get sued for not doing his due diligence. You watch, it'll be nothing to worry about."

"Yeah," I mutter, not wanting to let him know about the dark thoughts that have been circulating through my head since I left Todd's office. I try to remain calm, not wanting him to sense my apprehension. I need to know for certain before I say anything. "I'm sure that's all it is."

"Sounds like you need a distraction, pal."

He's not wrong; I desperately need to get out of my head. But football followed by a Monday night at the Stag's Head is not on the cards for me tonight, that much I'm completely sure about.

"I think I'm just gonna get an early night, mate," I reply, hoping it puts him off. "Can you let Bob know he will need to cover for me again? I'll make it up to him."

"Bob? Yes, no problem, I'll call him in a minute. But you're gonna want to hear this," he says, teasing me into giving in. "It's about your date-"

My pulse quickens, and my eyes widen. I forget all about the dreary doctor's appointment the second he mentions her. I sit myself up on the sofa, eager to hear more.

"Ella?" I ask, trying to remain calm. "Have you seen her?"

"Yes, pal. She came by the harbour looking for you a few hours ago."

"What did she say?" I ask him, unable to control my excitement. "Did she mention anything else?"

"Well, she was with a friend, but it did look like they'd walked down to find you on purpose," he says, and my heart skips a beat. "I asked if she wanted me to pass on a message, and she said just to let you know she'd stopped by and that she'd try and catch you another time."

My chest tightens, and a wave of heat rushes over me. I bite my lip and berate myself for not being there to speak to her. My heart races faster and faster with each thought.

"So?" Paul encourages.

"So what?" I ask, not sure what to say. Memories of Ella and the night we spent walking along the beach begin flooding my brain with happy thoughts.

"So, are you going to call her now? She's clearly interested in you."

"She hasn't got a phone, mate. I told you this at the pub last night."

"Oh yeah. Well, I'm sure you'll think of something," Paul laughs. "Anyway, gotta go, Beth's just got home, and we're off to the cinema after football practice. I would invite you, but a little bird tells me there's somewhere else you'd rather be."

I ponder his words, wondering if it would be weird for me to head over to Ella's house. I'm eager to see her in person and can't think of a better distraction.

"Enjoy your chick flick," I say to Paul, my voice sounding a little bit more upbeat now. "And thanks for calling - I appreciate it."

"Chick-flick my arse," Paul laughs. "Give me a call if you need picking up from the hospital on Wednesday."

I hang up the phone and let out a deep sigh. My body relaxes as I sink back into the soft cushions of the sofa. A quick glance at my watch confirms it's only 6 pm, still plenty of time to do something this evening if I choose to. But I have no idea what to do next.

I remain lying on the sofa for what feels like an age, staring at the photo of my parents and feeling torn between what the normal, reserved James would do and what James, with a possible death sentence, should do. I'm sure my dad would want me to make the most of my time, seeing as how precious it is, and there really is something about Ella that makes me desperate to see her again.

I stand up and rummage around the flat for a pen and some notepaper, eventually finding what I need on the bookcase between a Chris Kamara biography and an encyclopaedia on birds. Sweat beads across my forehead as I sit down and begin to write. It's weird, and I know it's not what people do nowadays with apps like Tinder making everything sexual within minutes of a match, but it used to be a romantic way to communicate. Ella's an author; I'm sure she will appreciate it.

I scribble my thoughts down, avoiding all mention of my doctor's appointment but letting her know that I haven't stopped thinking about her since we said goodbye at the book café. As much as I love reading, I've never been that great with words myself, so I just hope what I've written is enough to let her know that I want to spend more time with her. I slip it into an envelope, address it with her name, and seal it closed.

I glance back at the photo of my parents and wonder whether my dad would be proud of me. It's the first time in years that I've thought about him in this way, and the second-best thing I'm holding onto right now.

An hour passes, but to me, it seems like just a few minutes. I don't want to spend any more time in the flat - I feel restless, imprisoned and trapped by my own mind. I pull up the hood of my sweatshirt so I'm somewhat protected against the elements, grab a coat for an extra layer, and head outside, taking the letter with me.

My fingers reflexively reach for my car keys, but I stop myself. A bit of fresh air will do me good, and a walk is exactly what I need to clear my head.

I struggle across the street, bracing myself against the heavy wind and begin walking towards the outskirts of town. I've passed the cottage Ella is renting on the odd day trip I've made out to Staithes, and I know it's going to take me the best part of an hour to walk there, even if I up my pace.

My hands shake from the cold and with the anticipation of what I'm about to do. *Please, please let her find this romantic and not creepy,* I pray to no god in particular.

At last, I reach the hidden dirt path that leads the way up to her cottage. I navigate it carefully, using the faint light of my phone to do so - there are no streetlamps out here. The wind howls around me, and I can just make out the sound of waves crashing against the rocky shoreline, a noise that grows louder with each step I take.

I climb up and up the steep dirt drive, my bones aching with every step I take until the cottage comes into view, moonlight high-lighting its white stone walls against the inky sky. A light shines through the curtains in one of the rooms, drawing me towards it.

Should I knock? Just post the letter through the door and leave? Should I phone Beth and ask her which is the least creepy option?

My heart races as I pace closer and closer to the house. I remove the letter from my coat pocket and run my finger along the seal. Taking a deep breath, I clutch it firmly and walk towards the front door. I'm going to post it. As much as I want to see Ella tonight, turning up uninvited is more than a little weird, and a proper reunion with Jessica Beaver is not something I can handle this evening.

My heart skips a beat as I step onto the small stone path leading to the cottage's front door, and a motion sensor light is triggered, illuminating my position. I curse and hurry forward, wanting to post the letter and leave as quickly as possible.

I take longer strides and notice the curtains twitching just as I reach the letterbox on the old wooden door. I slide my letter through, my palms sweaty with nerves, but before I can drop it, the door opens just a touch.

"Hello there, stranger. Fancy seeing you here."

11

ELLA

"Just one moment," I say, my heart beating wildly as I take in the situation unfolding before me.

I push the door forwards to remove the latch and then open it wide again, giving James the space to enter. My landlord had been kind enough to stop by while I was in town with Jess this afternoon and had installed the security features I'd requested. Little did I realise that James would be the first to test them out.

"I didn't want to disturb you," James says as he shuffles into my small living room, his scuffed boots making a soft thud on the wooden floor. He's holding a folded envelope in one hand, and I'm instantly intrigued. "I, um, wrote you a letter and was just going to post it."

His cheeks flush a gentle pink, and he looks away shyly, almost as if embarrassed. His gaze falls on me, and in his eyes, I can see the same longing that he'd expressed the night at the book cafe.

My heart swells with emotion at the gesture, and I find myself unable to suppress a smile. "Thank you," I say softly as I take the envelope from him. Our fingers briefly brush against one another, and I feel a shiver run through me as an electric current seems to pass between us, warming my insides.

James turns to leave, but I find myself wanting him to stay. "Don't go," I plead, reaching out and touching his arm. His eyes glow in the light, and I can see a hint of a smile on his lips. Something about the way he looks at me gives me the courage to continue. "Would you like a drink? I don't think I've got anything alcoholic, but I've got coffee and a large selection of herbal teas."

My heart pounds in my chest, and my cheeks feel hot as I stand there, hoping for a positive response.

"A cup of tea would be great," James replies. "Is Jessica not here with you?"

"She's just having a long bath," I say, pointing my head towards the bathroom. "She takes forever in there. I honestly don't know how the water doesn't go cold."

James laughs, but I can tell he's feeling nervous. He clearly wasn't expecting his walk up here to lead to an invite inside.

I set the water on the stove to boil and sit down on the sofa, patting the cushion beside me, encouraging him to join me. James takes his coat off and sits down, and I can't help but feel a little bit excited about him being here with me. And I really want to know what's in the letter he wrote.

"So, you wrote me a letter, huh?" I ask, a genuine smile on my face. "Am I allowed to read it now, or would you prefer that I read it when I'm on my own?"

"Probably best to read it when you're alone," he chuckles. "I didn't expect to see you tonight, so I will probably embarrass myself if you read it in front of me."

My curiosity almost explodes with excitement, but I try my best to act cool. "Well, maybe you could give me a hint?" I whisper playfully, leaning close to him so he can hear every word.

"I, um, well, Paul phoned me earlier and said he'd seen you and Jessica at the harbour earlier today. And, honestly, I've been waiting for you to call me so I could have kicked myself when I wasn't there. I ended up looking at a photo of my mum and dad when they were probably about our age after I got off the phone, and although I never really knew my dad, I just felt like he was telling me to go for it and take a chance."

James stops talking and looks down at his hands. "I feel like that sounds a bit strange now that I've said it aloud."

My cheeks feel hot, and I'm eager to tell James just how much I appreciate him opening up to me and that I've been thinking the same thing. I want to kiss him and hug him and wrap my arms around his long, slender body. But at the same time, I feel nervous. I have so much going on in my life right now that I don't know how I feel about bringing somebody else into it. It wouldn't be fair for him to take all that on without knowing what he's getting into.

"James," I stammer breathlessly, touching his knee for reassurance. "I've been thinking about you a lot too. I really enjoyed our date the other night, and it was great getting to know you in the book cafe too. I just don't know if I'm ready for a relationship."

I look deep into his eyes, and he nods at me, an acceptance falling over his features.

"It's not you, it's me, right?" he smiles a sad smile.

"Not exactly," I say. "Let me get our drinks, and I'll try to explain."

I scurry around the kitchen, my heart racing as I fill two mugs with steaming hot tea. I try to compose myself before returning to the living room with a mug in each hand and passing James his. My hands cling to the warmth of the porcelain as I search for the right words to explain my chaotic existence to the handsome man who sits before me.

"You don't have to tell me, Ella," James says to me thoughtfully. "I meant it when I said I was happy just being friends."

"I do," I reply. "I want to tell you so that you understand. It's just a lot, and I'm trying to figure out where to start."

"Aren't you an author?" he chuckles, and I can't help but laugh.

"Not a very good one, clearly," I say.

James places a hand on my knee and squeezes it gently. "Just tell me as much or as little as you want me to know."

I sigh and try to collect my thoughts. Even just thinking about what I've gone through makes my anxiety rear its ugly head. But I don't want him leaving feeling that my inaction is somehow down to him because he couldn't be any further from the truth.

"Ok," I say, taking a deep breath. "So, I said at the book cafe that I was visiting Whitby for an extended stay. That's not exactly the whole story."

"Go on," he says, picking up his mug and taking a long sip of warm tea. I do the same, the hot liquid warming my stomach and helping to push my fears away.

"Well, the extended version is that I moved here to escape my old life. After my first book became a bestseller, I was offered a contract and an advance for more books, and I couldn't have been happier. But that happiness didn't last long. A man - I assume it's just one anyway - started seeking me out and making me feel like utter shit at every turn.

I'd wake up in the morning to dozens of emails, hundreds of notifications on social media, and fake reviews created by profiles that had been set up the day the reviews were left, and that's not even mentioning all the fake social media profiles he'd set up in my name or the newsletters he'd sign me up for. And don't think I didn't change my email either because I did - multiple times. Somehow, he kept finding out what I was doing.

That was all bad enough, but I soon started to feel like he was watching my every move. If I visited my publisher, he knew about it. If I did a library signing, he would email me with specifics that he couldn't have known about if he hadn't been there.

Jess knew about some of it, and she tried to help me work out who it was, but no one stood out. My publisher didn't seem overly concerned. I also filed a police report, but they basically told me I had no case, so closed it. Before I left my old home, things were so bad that I hardly ever left my flat. I began to think it was my fault that this was happening and my fault for letting it get so bad. But every notification that came through to my phone left me in a complete state of panic, and I'd struggle to breathe or sleep unless I drank myself into oblivion."

James takes my hand in his and squeezes it gently, his brown eyes full of compassion and understanding. I can feel his support before he's even spoken a word, which gives me the courage to continue.

"After a particularly bad day in which I downed two bottles of red wine in the space of an hour and couldn't have made it to the shop for more even if I'd wanted to, I realised I needed to sort myself out. Nobody else was going to be able to help me fix this; I needed to do it on my own. So, I forced myself to open up my laptop and log in to the author Discord I'd joined back in the day. That's when I found this place. I booked it without giving it any thought other than whether I could afford it and being too drunk to care about whether it was a good decision or not. Four days later, I packed my belongings, hired a small removal van and moved.

I didn't tell anybody. And when I got here, I turned my phone off and threw it in a drawer so nobody could contact me either."

My chest heaves as I fill my lungs with air and stare straight into James' eyes, willing him to know that I'd said as much as I could.

"You didn't even let Jessica know?" he asks, the concern evident on his face.

"I didn't let anybody know," I confirm.

"And that explains the lack of a phone," he says, realisation hitting him.

"Yes," I say. "I've found a way around that now, and I'm happy to give you my new number, but until Jess got here, well, I didn't feel able to-"

James reaches forward and pulls me into a tight embrace. I close my eyes and let the tears flow freely as I feel his strong arms wrap around me in comfort. I can feel his steady breath against my hair, reassuring me that he understands and isn't going anywhere.

"Ella, I really think you need to go to the police," James says as he wipes a tear from my face.

"I've been saying the same thing," a voice from the other side of the room calls out. I look up, and Jess is hobbling over to us, wrapped in a lopsided bath towel. She looks pretty annoyed at the intrusion, and I can't help but laugh. "She won't listen to me, so maybe you can talk some sense into her."

"I've tried before, Jess, you know I have," I plead, knowing it won't get me anywhere. "I filed a report in York, and they closed the case."

"That was before everything else that's happened, Ella," she says as she flops down into the armchair across from us.

"There's more?" James asks.

I glance down at the once steaming cup of tea, now lukewarm and no longer comforting. A chill runs down my spine, and I shiver, not sure how much more I can explain. I look at Jess, and she frowns but takes the hint that I'd prefer her to continue my story.

"A few hours before Ella went out with you, she contacted me," Jess continues, "to let me know she was still alive. And I'm still not okay with your decision to just up and leave without saying a word, missy! But anyway, she had to turn her old phone on to get my number, and she'd received a ton of new messages in the few days she'd been offline."

I look at her, silently pleading with her not to tell James about my panic attack.

"The messages had been getting worse," Jess continues. "They were almost insinuating that this man knew where she was. He knew she'd left York, and he told her that she'd regret it and that he would find her."

"Jesus," James responds, pushing his hand through his thick dark hair.

"Yeah, so Ella quickly wrote my number down and turned her phone back off. Next thing she knows, a man is standing by the window telling her he said he'd find her. She phones me, freaking out, crying, not sure whether she's safe or not, and I tell her I'll drive over, and we'll sort this mess out."

I look at James and can see he's trying to make sense of all this information he's had forced upon him. I feel my palms getting sweaty and wonder if telling him all this was a mistake.

"So, wait," he responds, looking at me. "The night we went out, you were dealing with all this and didn't think you could tell me?"

"Sorry," I reply. "I was already acting like the weirdest date you've probably ever had. I didn't think you needed all of my drama on top."

"And can I just say," Jess adds, butting in, "that even though you had no idea what was going on, I appreciate you staying with Ella until I arrived. You have no idea how much of a relief it was to find her still there, and with someone I knew too."

James pushes his fingers through his hair again, and I'm grateful when Jess offers to get us both another mug of tea. I watch as she leaves the room and turn back to James.

"It was my pleasure to stay with you that night," he tells me once we're alone. "I really did enjoy your company."

"I'm so sorry," I say. "I didn't think I should tell you all of this at the cafe, but for what it's worth, I had a great evening too, and you helped to take my mind off this mess the whole time we were there."

James wraps his strong arms around me, and I can't help but melt against his chest again, feeling the gentle thump of his heart and the warmth radiating from his body. His embrace is full of love, making my whole body relax.

"You have nothing to apologise for," he says.

Jess opens the door and pushes a mug into my hand before apologising for interrupting our embrace. James pulls away, but I can tell he doesn't want to.

"I hope you are going to listen to us," Jess says, annoyed. "I'm leaving in a couple of days, and I would feel so much better if I knew the police were aware of what's been going on."

"I know, but-"

"No buts," she interrupts. "This man has found you, Ella. Trust me when I say he won't give up."

"Was it the same man who made you uneasy at the cafe?" James asks, suddenly remembering.

"I don't know," I reply honestly. "I didn't see his face at the window. He stood with his back to me. I didn't know if it was a coincidence, or if it was the same man, or even what was going on."

"I see," James responds, and I feel his body stiffen.

"It probably was the same man," Jess interjects. "From what I remember of Ella's account of the night, he had to have been watching, waiting for a moment like that."

"But I'm just baffled that no one has managed to get any information on him," James says.

"The police didn't have anything to go on in York," I reply. "All of the emails were sent using a VPN, and they couldn't find the true owners of the social media accounts either. I know he was watching me, but I never had any proof. I just started to think I was paranoid."

"You're not paranoid, Ella," Jess says. "I'm sorry if I made you feel that way."

I smile at her thankfully. "I was in such a bad place towards the end of my time there. I was pushing everyone away."

"Have things been better since you got here?" James asks. "Aside from the intrusion last Thursday, I mean?"

"Yeah," I reply. "They honestly have. Jess helped me set up a new phone. You and everyone else in the town have made me feel really welcome. And I don't feel compelled to drink two bottles of wine to get to sleep every night."

"Well," James says, holding my hands and looking at Jess. "If Ella isn't ready to speak to the police just yet, I think it should be her call. I'm happy to check in on her as often as she needs me to once you're back home, and," he looks at me, "I'd love to introduce you properly to Paul and Beth too, so you can get to know people around here. Whoever this guy is, he won't have the same kind of luck stalking you in Whitby as he had in York. Everybody knows everybody here, and I can put the word out."

"Thank you," I say, genuinely grateful for his kindness.

Jess sighs and slowly stands up. "I just want what's best for you, Ella," she says, tapping my shoulder gently as she leaves the room.

I melt into James' body and lean against his chest. His arms wrap around me, holding me tightly as I listen to the beat of his heart.

"I just want what's best for you too," he replies. I relax as he plays with the ends of my hair with one of his hands before kissing the top of my head.

For the first time in months, I feel like I'm making the right decision and that I have people here supporting me.

I tilt my head back and look up at James, his lips inches away from mine. His dark eyes stare deep into me as if trying to read all my hidden thoughts.

Slowly he lowers his mouth onto mine until we are kissing each other tenderly, passionately exploring every inch of our souls through touch and taste. As I kiss him, I'm filled with a warmth that radiates throughout me, pushing all my negative thoughts and demons away.

James pulls away slightly but keeps us connected forehead-to-forehead as he speaks softly. "No matter what happens, Ella, you can always count on me. I promise things will improve, and you won't have to live in fear anymore."

I want to stay like this forever, wrapped up in the security of James' arms and basking in his warmth. But alas, Jess interrupts us again.

"Thank you for everything," I whisper as he stands to leave.

"Promise me you will call or text if you need anything?" he says as Jess returns to the guest room, and I agree wholeheartedly, my heart racing. I quickly write my new number down on a piece of paper and give it to him.

"Do you want a ride home, James?" Jess calls, her voice cheerful and genuine. I can't help but be happy about how at ease she is around him too, even if it is a bit crazy that they knew each other back in the day.

"No thanks," he shouts in reply. "The fresh air will do me good. Catch you later."

I kiss him a soft goodbye and watch as he walks back out into the night.

12

JAMES

I push through the heavy glass doors of the hospital, the smell of antiseptic hitting me instantly as I enter the lobby. My feet drag with exhaustion, and my head throbs as I approach the reception. I've had a pretty uncomfortable 36 hours since I left Ella's cottage. The medication Dr Todd prescribed did its job, but I've barely been able to leave the confines of my small bathroom while it worked its way through me. Still, the evening I'd spent with Ella kept me going, and it gave me something other than my health issues to focus on.

We've been texting quite a lot since she gave me her number, my thumbs racing over the keys as we exchanged as much info as we could with each other. I hadn't, however, told her anything to do with my health concerns. She had enough to be dealing with right now, and I didn't want to make her worry about me if there was a chance she didn't need to.

I check in at reception and am directed to a waiting room full of identical wooden chairs, each one sporting its own blue and orange checked cushion. Orderly, uniform. How many people have sat here before me waiting to be told that life as they know it is coming to an end?

I take a deep breath and slowly lower myself into a chair, my stomach churning with nerves. I nervously fiddle with my phone before finally pressing the button to switch it off, not wanting anything to disturb me for the next two hours.

"Mr Clarke?" a nurse calls out from the opposite side of the waiting room.

I move to stand up, and she gives me a warm, friendly smile.

"We can take you through to a room now if you'd like to follow me?"

I nod, putting my phone back in my pocket.

The nurse leads me down a corridor, my shoes squeaking against the waxed linoleum floor. We enter a small room, and she places her hand on the small of my back, indicating for me to sit down in one of the two chairs that have been set up ready for the appointment. I watch as she takes a seat in a well-worn swivel chair and crosses her legs, her gaze trained on me.

"I'm Nurse Smith," she says, holding up a clipboard and smiling. "Before we start, I just need to go through a few things with you."

I nod, clenching my fists as I try to calm my nerves and hoping against all hope that everything will be ok.

"So, once the doctor arrives, we'll ask you to get undressed and lie on your side on the bed over there." She points towards a bed in the room, and I swallow nervously. "The procedure itself shouldn't hurt, but it may feel slightly uncomfortable when we pump the air to open your bowels. Now, we have a few different things here that you can take to make yourself more comfortable. There's standard parac-etamol or gas and air-"

Nurse Smith continues to talk, and I begin to zone out. I feel like I'm going to start hyperventilating. It's not the procedure; it's every-thing. My dad likely sat in this exact same chair, listening to the exact same spiel, only to be told he had weeks, or possibly months, left to live. How am I supposed to sit here and listen to all this talk about feeling comfortable when I know this is the beginning of the end?

"Mr Clarke?" the nurse says, placing her hand on my arm and shaking me out of my thoughts. "Is everything ok?"

My cheeks flush hot, and my palms are slick with sweat as I

nervously glance around the room. I mumble an apology with a shaky voice before using my hand to wipe the moisture from my forehead. "Um, sorry, where were we again?"

"I was just asking if you'd take a look at these forms and sign at the bottom if you're happy with everything," she says in a calm voice, handing me the clipboard she'd been holding earlier.

I grit my teeth, barely glancing at the papers she places in front of me. I sign quickly, not wanting to waste any more time and hand them back. I watch as she nods in acknowledgement before turning away and tapping away at the computer in the room.

"Did you decide which pain relief you'd prefer?" she asks, turning back towards me again. "Most people opt for gas and air, but we can give you a sedative if you'd prefer. You'll just have to get someone to drive you home after the procedure if you opt for that."

"Gas and air is fine," I murmur.

I press my shaking hands into the cool leather of the exam room chair, my heart pounding so loud I'm surprised the nurse can't hear it. I watch absentmindedly as her fingertips hover over the keyboard before typing a few more notes.

"Ok, well, the doctor will be here in a moment. Is there anything else you'd like to ask while we've got a few minutes?" she asks, turning back to face me with a warm smile.

I wrap my arms around myself for comfort and shake my head quickly.

"Ok. I'll need you to pop on this hospital gown before the doctor arrives. There's a curtain just over there, and you'll find a chair to leave your clothes on. If you need anything, just let me know."

I do as she says, my body moving almost on autopilot.

A few minutes later, a light knock echoes through the room, and I watch as Nurse Smith gets up to let the doctor in. A middle-aged gentleman with salt and pepper hair and a pair of wire-framed glasses enters the room. I watch as he speaks to the nurse in hushed tones before inviting me to get up onto the bed. I fold my clothes neatly and place them on the chair before doing as he asks.

"A colonoscopy is a simple procedure," he tells me, "and it

shouldn't take much longer than 30 minutes. You may feel a little bit uncomfortable, but Nurse Smith is setting up the nitrous oxide for you now, so do take some deep breaths on that if you need to."

I turn to my side, feeling self-conscious in the skimpy hospital gown I'm being forced to wear, and watch as the nurse demonstrates how to use the funny-looking contraption beside me.

"If you feel like it's too much at any point, let me or Nurse Smith know, and we can stop," the doctor says. "As I said, you shouldn't feel anything painful except for maybe the odd stomach cramp and a bit of bloating."

I nod, really wanting to get this over with quickly.

"Ok, get yourself into position, and we'll begin."

I feel the firm yet gentle grip of Nurse Smith as she helps to move me into the correct position before handing me the gas and air tube. I hold it in a vice-like grip, my knuckles turning white with every passing second, and take a breath to make sure it's working. I don't think it is, but it helps to have something to focus on.

A quick glance up tells me that the nurse has moved to stand beside the doctor, and I'm glad not to have to face anyone while they perform the procedure. I close my eyes as they start and will it all to be over quickly.

FORTY MINUTES LATER, and it's all done. I want to get dressed and leave, my embarrassment fully getting the better of me, but Nurse Smith encourages me to remain lying down for a little while.

"We just want to make sure you're ok before you leave," she says, patting my arm for reassurance.

"Did you find anything?" I ask her, not really wanting to know the answer but feeling uncomfortable just lying here in silence.

"Yes," she replies, and my heart sinks. "There were a few polyps, which the doctor removed, and we've also taken a sample of cells which we'll send for testing in the lab. The results will be sent to your GP, and you should hear from him within two to three weeks."

"Is it cancer?" I ask, my heart rate quickening at the thought.

"We won't know for certain until the test results come back from the lab, but if it helps make you feel better, very few results come back positive. Benign growths are more common than you'd think."

She smiles at me like I have nothing to worry about, and honestly, I feel a bit better with that knowledge. Maybe I've been overthinking things. Just because my dad died of bowel cancer, that doesn't mean my fate is set and sealed. Like Paul said, Dr Todd was probably just being cautious, knowing my family history. That's all it is. *It can't be anything more.*

I push my hands through my hair and take a few deep breaths to calm myself down properly. There's nothing I can do now except wait, and at least I have Ella here to distract me. Gorgeous, amazing Ella, who deserves so much more than life has thrown her way over the last year.

I push myself into a sitting position and listen as the nurse explains what to expect over the next 24 hours. It doesn't sound too bad, but a night at home with a takeaway in front of the TV sounds like the best plan. My stomach rumbles loudly, and I can't help but think about how hungry I am. Fasting is not something I'll be doing again in a hurry.

"Do you have anybody coming to give you a ride home?" Nurse Smith asks me.

I was considering calling Paul to give me a lift home, but a quick look at my watch tells me he'll still be on the boat, and I don't want to hang around here any longer than I have to.

"No," I reply. "I was just planning on calling a taxi."

She looks me over one last time and types a few last notes into the computer. "I don't see any reason why you can't leave when you're ready," she says. "Just take it easy for a couple of days and give us a call if you notice a high temperature, severe stomach pain, or have a lot of bleeding. All being well, you'll be back to your normal life in a couple of days."

I thank her and slide off the bed before dressing myself again and leaving the way I came.

THE CLOCK on the wall chimes five o'clock. I've been lounging on the couch since I got home, half-heartedly watching a show about cars on Netflix that I'm having trouble concentrating on. My gaze shifts from the television to my phone on the coffee table, and I wonder if I should call Ella. I know Jess is planning to go home today, and I want to check in with her and ensure she's ok, but I don't want to interrupt any last moments with her best friend either.

Cursed with indecision, I do nothing but sit and wait, letting my mind wander and hoping I'll hear from her soon.

13

ELLA

"Hey, Ella! James must have dropped by and posted another letter. I've just noticed one on the doormat. There's no stamp again. He really does like you, doesn't he?"

I quickly stop cutting tomatoes for our salad as Jess shouts me, excited to read what James has written this time. His last letter was so beautiful that I'd read it repeatedly, never tiring of its romantic words. The edges had started to fold, though, so I'm happy to have a new one to obsess over.

I peer out of the window, the night sky slowly darkening, as I search for a sign of James. Yet it appears I'm too late. Resigned, I cross the room and take the letter from Jess's hands, fingering it nervously.

"Aren't you going to open it?" she laughs. "I don't know, Ella, you move to a new town, and you've already got somebody sending you hand-delivered love letters. I'd love to know how you do it."

I smile and feel heat rise to my cheeks. Jess's eyes are on me, but I feel a bit uncomfortable reading it in front of her. James' first letter was quite personal, and I expect this one will be the same. I don't want to share that with anybody else. Not even my best friend.

"I'll read it tonight," I say, tucking the envelope into my pocket.

"It'll give me something to look forward to after my best friend leaves me."

I mimic someone dying of a broken heart, and she pushes me playfully.

"Give over, Ella; I'm not that far away. Plus, you're the one who upped and left. It should be me making you feel bad, not the other way around."

I return to the kitchen and add the tomatoes I'd sliced to the bowl filled with lettuce, grated carrots and a generous helping of cucumber. I splash some dressing over the top and give it one final mix before picking up the bowl and turning to Jess.

"Done," I say triumphantly. "Let's go eat our final meal."

"You could have picked something more exciting than salad," she laughs while helping me through to the dining room with plates and cutlery.

"If I could get around the marketplace without feeling like I have to buy half the goods on the fruit and veg stall, I would have done," I laugh.

We take our seats at the table, and I can't help but feel sad about Jess leaving.

"I can't believe how quickly this last week has gone," I say before shoving a forkful of lettuce into my mouth.

"Are you sure you're going to be ok once I leave?" Jess asks, the familiar look of concern clear on her face.

"Yes, honestly," I reply. "You've helped me set up a new phone, and I think I'm going to ask James if he wants to meet up again." My heart quickens as I think of him, and I struggle to suppress a smile. The universe is clearly giving me some good karma right now.

"Do you want me to keep your old phone?" she asks. "I'm happy to keep dealing with the messages so you don't have to look at them."

"Have I been getting a lot still?" I ask, my chest suddenly tightening.

Jess doesn't answer me, so I know the answer to that. I wish I could switch off from it entirely, but I can't.

"You can tell me, Jess," I press.

"If anything, he seems to be getting worse," she replies, looking forlorn. "The emails have been getting more..."

"More what?" I ask, needing to know.

"More threatening Ella."

"Shit. Does he know where I am?"

"I don't know. The emails aren't exactly written in a way that makes much sense."

I know what she means. They'd started out looking like standard fan mail, but when I stopped replying, they became more disjointed and messy. Some of them were hard to make any sense of at all.

I ponder whether to let Jess take my phone back to York with her or not. On the one hand, I felt a lot better not having the messages invade my mind, but on the other, it was hard to ignore them entirely, not knowing what he might do next.

"Are you sure you don't mind reading them?" I ask her. "It's a lot to deal with."

"If this is what it takes to get the old Ella back, I am happy to do it," Jess confirms.

"Ok, well, I'd really appreciate it if you're alright with it. Just let me know if things start getting worse, yeah? If he's definitely found out where I've moved to or you think I'm in danger, I need to know."

"God honey, if it's looking like that's likely, I'll be right back here, and I'll be phoning the police too. I know you want to keep them out of it, but your safety is all that matters to me right now."

"Thanks, Jess," I say, grateful for everything she's doing for me.

Despite knowing he hasn't stopped emailing, I'm not feeling as bad did before I moved here. A proper break from my old phone has done me a world of good, and I can't help but think how much easier life would have been in the days before technology became so integrated into our lives.

"I'm so proud of you," she says, smiling at me and squeezing my hand. "You've been through such a hard time, and as much as I'd love to feel sorry for myself for losing you, I know you've done the right thing moving here."

"I'm really glad you were able to come and visit," I reply, my heart swelling with happiness as I think again of how much she's done for me. "I really appreciate all you're doing for me. I just wish..." I pause and shake my head. "I just wish it was under better circumstances."

"It will happen," she says cheerfully. "Honestly, Ella, give it six months, and we'll be doing this again - hopefully when you've made friends with a butcher so we can have burgers instead of salad - and everything will look so much brighter. I love you more than anyone else in the world, and I promise I'll make sure you find yourself again."

We sit in comfortable silence as we eat the last of our lunch, the sound of the sea against the rocks outside providing the perfect backdrop. Once we've eaten and I've tidied the plates away, Jess returns to the guest room and packs up the rest of her stuff.

My eyes sting as I watch Jess pull away in her car. "Text me," she shouts as she reverses. "I want to hear about everything - don't leave a girl hanging!"

I laugh and promise that I will, trying not to let my tears fall until she's out of eyesight.

I take a few deep breaths as I watch her car disappear down the road and try to focus on the positives in my life now. I'm going to go inside, make a pot of hot tea, and give James a call. I haven't texted him at all today, not wanting Jess to think I was distracted by him on her last day here, and the anticipation has been killing me. I'm almost giddy with anticipation.

I take the water off the stove and pour myself a mug of tea, adding just a dash of milk at the end before carrying it through into the living room. My fingers itch as I wait for my phone to power on. Finally, with a trembling hand, I click the call button, and James answers on the second ring.

"Hello there, stranger. Fancy hearing from you this evening," he says. My heart races at the sound of his voice, and I try to calm my nerves, sound like the cool girl I've always wanted to be.

"Hey yourself. Good day?"

"Yeah, not bad. You? Has Jessica left now?"

"Yup," I reply. "I've just seen her off. Feels weird without her here."

"I can imagine," he says, his warm laugh rippling down the line. "Who would have thought I'd end up having the hots for Jessica Beaver's best friend?"

"Ha, you are so going to have to let me know what she was like at school," I reply. Jess hadn't mentioned much about her childhood to me really. I knew she grew up in Whitby but then couldn't wait to leave when she turned 16, but that was about it. She'd been feeling nostalgic for the place in recent months, which is probably what helped me decide to move here.

"Ah, she was a strange kid. I didn't know her super well. Different friendship groups, you know. I'm glad she made something good of her life, in any case. So, what does she think about you moving back here? Is it a bit weird for her?"

"Nah, I don't think so," I reply. "She told me just before she left that she thought I'd made a good decision. She enjoyed her few days away, too, so I'm hoping she'll come back and visit again soon."

We talk for what seems like hours, and I end up drinking the entire pot of tea I'd made. We laugh, share stories, and so easily connect that it feels like we're old friends that have known each other all our lives.

"I meant to ask you," James says after I've just finished telling him a random story about a pet woodlouse I kept as a kid. "Would you be up for a night out on Sunday? The Stag's Head has a pub quiz, and I usually go with Paul and Beth. I'd love for you to join us, and I'm sure Beth will love having something other than fishing and the footie to talk about."

"Sure, that sounds wonderful," I say, my eyes twinkling with amusement. "You know, authors are actually quite the trivia buffs? We do so much research to make sure the facts we put into our books are accurate that our brains end up storing a wealth of useless information. It's a natural talent."

James laughs hard. "We could definitely do with some talent. Unless the questions are about fish, old video games, or celebrities, we have no clue what we're doing."

I can't help but laugh back. "What time shall I meet you?" I ask.

"We usually meet around seven," he replies. "But I'm happy to pick you up if it's easier. That way, you can have a drink if you want to. It's normally pretty busy in there, especially if the football crowd is still drinking, but Beth usually rocks up early to save us a table."

"Ok, sure," I reply. "I'll make sure I'm ready for you. I'm looking forward to it."

We say our goodbyes, and I have a massive smile on my face as I click off my phone, heat rushing through my body to my chest. It's been a tough year, but I can't help but feel like things are starting to get better, and I have James and Jess to thank for that.

I take a quick shower and briskly towel dry my hair and body before wrapping a robe around myself and walking through to the bedroom. I'm going to get dry and dressed and then snuggle up in bed with James' latest letter. Strangely, I feel a pang of disappointment that he hadn't mentioned stopping by with it when I called. But I remind myself of how thoughtful he is in general. He probably just didn't want to disturb my last day with Jess.

14

JAMES

The early morning sunlight glints off the edges of the boat as I step onto the deck, and I savour the smell of salt in the air. Paul gives me a wave from where he's making some last-minute repairs on the railing, and despite not feeling 100%, it feels good to be working together again.

Paul has been stressed lately, trying to get enough money together for his wedding, and with me having taken most of the week off due to my hospital appointment, it just made sense to try and earn some extra cash. We'd done a few tourist charters last year, and they'd proven really popular, so we decided to start our little side business again on the odd weekend. It was double or nothing, but it was worth it.

"Now then, mate. Good to see you again," Paul shouts as I climb aboard the boat. We tried to make it look a bit more comfortable when we had guests aboard, but it wasn't working so well. There's not much you can do to make old fishing nets and tarps look good.

"Ay up," I say as I walk over and help him. "Who have you managed to book today, then?"

"Well, it was pretty last minute, mate, so we've got a couple of newlyweds visiting Whitby for their honeymoon and a man I met down the pub last night. Still, it'll be a good trial for when we take bigger groups of people out as the season picks up, eh?"

"Aye," I reply. "A trial run sounds good."

Paul spots our guests moving along the dock and waves to them. "Welcome aboard," he says as he helps our customers across the gangplank. "This is the 'Cray Cray Fish', and it's where you'll be spending the next few hours, so make yourselves at home. There's a bathroom over there, a few seats towards the front of the boat, and I've packed a few snacks and drinks in the ice cooler just there. Help yourself to anything you need."

He points to a box next to my feet, and I open it to show them, half wondering why he thought beer was a good idea.

"Life jackets are just here," he says, continuing the talk. "I can't force you to wear one, but I highly recommend that you do. It might look calm here at the harbour, but it can get really choppy as we head out to sea."

All of our customers hold their hands out, accepting a life jacket. The man on his own pauses for a second as though he has something to say but thinks better of it.

"Let me give you a quick rundown of what to expect today, and then we can leave," Paul continues. "We'll take you around some of the big landmarks in the bay before we head down south a bit to our favourite local fishing spot. We've got all the gear here ready for you, and you're welcome to keep any fish you catch. If you're lucky, you may even catch a big seabass-"

I leave Paul to it, out of earshot of our customers, and watch as they stand on the other side of the boat, drinks in hand. The pale-faced man on his own looks up and catches me looking at him. His eyes remind me of a man I knew long ago, but his face is hard to place. Maybe he's been on another boat I worked on. It wouldn't be the first time I've had tourists who look familiar.

"Alright, we're ready to leave," Paul shouts over to me.

I tug on the lines, loosening them from the dock cleats and

sending them tumbling into a heap on the boat's deck. With a push of the ignition button, the engine roars to life, startling the couple for a second. I smile at them, letting them know there's nothing to worry about, and then carefully pull back on the throttle, guiding the boat out of the harbour and past the breakwater, just far enough so that we can see the first landmark on our trip.

Paul eagerly steps up to the task of being the boat's tour guide. He's way better at it than I am, and I'm lost in my own thoughts today. My stomach twists with excitement about finally seeing Ella again tonight, but I can't help but notice that she's been a little 'off' with me in her messages the last couple of days. Despite letting me know about her crazy fan, she still seems guarded, many of her messages to me short and clipped.

I glance down at my mobile, the signal starting to wane the further out to sea we get, and decide to turn it off. She hasn't initiated any conversations since she called the other night, and I'm tired of trying to work out what I said that could have hurt her. I'll see her in a few hours, so I can ask her then.

I pull the boat up to the second landmark, and Paul continues spouting his seemingly endless stream of information. The couple in the front seats have pretty much twisted themselves into a single person, wholly engrossed in each other despite Paul's best efforts to keep everyone's attention.

Ugh, can everyone stop having such perfect love lives, please?

I look around the boat and notice the pale-faced man frowning and rolling his eyes at their overt display of affection, and I'm glad I'm not the only one thinking it's a bit much. I glance at Paul, and he shrugs at me, an exasperated sigh leaving his lips.

Not even waiting for Paul to finish his usual spiel, I turn the motor back on and zoom towards the fishing spot. At least once we're there, I can stop focusing on the happy couple sitting right in my eye line and direct my attention back to the sea, the one thing I can always rely on to keep me calm.

"I'm here for a trip out, not to be a third party in some cheesy love story," the man on his own says as he joins me at the boat's wheel. "I'm Leonard, by the way."

"James," I say and shake his hand.

"If you ask me, I'd say you need to start vetting your customers."

"Yeah, starting to think the same thing," I reply. The couple in front of us are practically on top of each other now, and it's becoming rude.

Paul comes to join us, shaking his head. "We nearly at the fishing spot yet, mate?"

"Yup, just pulling up to it now," I say, the relief clear on my face.

As I turn the motor off, Paul rushes to grab our rods while I scramble to line up a few chairs along the boat's interior.

I sit down and start loading my rod with bait. Leonard sits in the chair next to me and watches intently as I attach a sinker to the line, cast it out into the clear blue waters and let it drift.

"Do you fish regularly?" he asks, his voice slightly more relaxed now that we have reached our destination and no longer have to watch as the happy couple shows us just how in love they are.

I nod in response before Paul cuts in: "He's been fishing for as long as I've known him! He knows this area like no other."

We talk about past fishing trips we've taken together until, finally, there's a tug on my line; a big seabass on the end of it. I start reeling in, but the rope is caught on something. I look over at Paul, and he motions to tell me the line's tangled. I try and reel harder, but my heart drops when the fish breaks free.

"Ha, fishing's not your thing then?" Leonard chuckles.

"Doesn't look like it today," I shrug. I try to continue a conversation, but my mind keeps straying back to Ella and how I could have upset her. Our phone call went as well as it could have done in my mind, and now I can't help thinking I'm an inconsiderate ass despite having absolutely zero clue as to why.

"So, you never did let me know how you got on at the hospital," Paul says as he sits down on my other side, beer in hand.

"Oh, you know," I say, not wanting to open up too much in front of a customer. "It was fine, I guess. Just waiting to hear more now."

"Any idea when that will be?" Paul asks, a frown on his face.

"I've got an appointment with Todd in the morning. Guess I'll be given my death sentence then. It's first thing, so I shouldn't be too late to work in the morning."

"My dad used to work at the local community hospital," Leonard chimes in before Paul can respond. "Not in a big doctor role or anything; he was a porter. Mum had to pretty much convince him to retire though he loved it that much."

"You're from around here, then?" Paul asks.

"Used to be," Leonard replies. "I moved away for a few years but came back a couple of months ago to help my dad care for my mum. Dementia. Gets you fast."

"I'm sorry to hear that," Paul says kindly. "I lost me mam when I was young, and James here lost his dad when he was a baby. It's hard, but your dad's lucky to have you supporting him."

Leonard's mouth curves into a timid smile, but his eyes remain glassy and still. I can tell from the way his jaw is clenched and the tension in his shoulders that this is something he's struggling to accept. I pat him on the knee in comfort, not having any words of my own to share.

We check our lines and cast out again into the ocean. I take a deep breath, praying for at least one bite. I need this. Luckily, I don't have to wait long as I feel a sharp tug on my line. I pull back hard, my rod bending with the weight of some unseen creature beneath the surface. Finally, after a few minutes of struggling against each other, and with Paul's help, the bass breaches the waves and flops onto the boat. I smile wide, feeling a triumphant rush of adrenaline as it clings to the railing.

"Well done, mate," Paul congratulates me. "I knew you had it in you."

Leonard gives me a firm tap on the back, his smile still stilted from our earlier conversation.

I dispatch the fish quickly and clean and gut it while we're on the boat. Leonard watches me with interest, and I can't help but feel proud of my skills. I place it in an ice box when I'm done and stand up, a big grin on my face.

"That was pretty impressive, man," Leonard says, patting me on the back again.

"Cheers," I reply. "Hey, why don't you take that fish back with you? Enjoy it with your old man tonight."

"Oh, I couldn't," Leonard says, taking a step back. "It's been great fishing with you, but I can't accept this."

"You're our customer," Paul says, taking a swig of beer. "Take it. It's not often he's this generous."

Leonard stutters in response but eventually accepts the fish. He smiles broadly as he lifts it up and holds it next to his head like an oversized party hat.

"You're a good man, James," he says, looking over to the happy couple, who are still more interested in each other than the fishing trip they signed up for. "You deserve better."

His comment makes me blush. I didn't realise I'd been making my jealousy quite so clear.

As we pull back to the harbour, Leonard shakes mine and Paul's hands before thanking us again for a great day on the water. Paul has to pretty much turf our other two customers off the boat, and I can't help but feel a little bit annoyed at how they acted.

"Idiots," Paul says once they're finally out of earshot.

"Ha, that'll be you and Beth once you finally tie the knot," I jest.

"Keep giving away all our good catches, and that won't be happening any time soon," Paul replies. "Anyway, you up for the quiz tonight? I know you weren't feeling it last week, but it could be fun."

"About that-"

"Don't tell me you're cancelling on us," Paul pleads. "Seriously, Beth's been looking forward to it all week. She's been desperate to make sure you're ok for herself. Doesn't trust me to check up on you properly."

I can't help but laugh.

"Calm down, mate; I'm coming. I'm going to bring Ella along too, if that's alright?"

"Great!" Paul replies, and I find I'm feeling excited about seeing her again.

"I said I'd pick her up, so we'll be there around 7. Catch you later mate."

"Look after yourself, J," he replies.

15

ELLA

I add the final touches to my makeup before running mascara over my eyelashes. This is the first time I've properly dressed up to go out with James, and I'm wondering if I've overdone it a bit. We've hardly spoken since I phoned him four days ago and I've been having second thoughts about whether going out with him again is a good idea.

I mean, we get on great in person, and it would be good to meet some new friends here, but his last letter has made me reconsider everything I thought about him.

Tiptoeing to the window, I push aside the yellowing curtains and squint at the night sky—no sign of headlights or stars, only an impenetrable curtain of darkness. I watch the hands on the antique clock in the living room, their slow movements barely registering a change in time, and the minutes drag until I finally hear the rumble of a car engine.

I grab my purse and my keys and lock up quickly, rushing over to James as he opens the car door for me.

"Evening, beautiful," he says as I step into the car, and I can't help but blush. "Ready for the best Sunday night out Whitby has to offer?"

The scent of expensive cologne fills the car. Mixed with the smell of upholstery and car exhaust, it makes my head spin, and I'm forced to open a window to catch my breath. "I am," I reply, squeezing my purse tightly against me as I try to remain calm. "This will be my first pub quiz in over a decade."

I look over at James and can't help but notice how good-looking he is. He's wearing a navy jumper that accentuates his well-toned physique and a pair of light jeans that look like they've been freshly ironed. I wonder if that's intentional. His hair is still messy, but a styled kind of messy, and he looks good. Really good, in fact! I let out a long breath before looking out the window and settling back into my seat.

"Yeah, I guess there are much better ways to spend evenings in York, right?" James laughs. "Good restaurants, the theatre, music gigs. Whitby does seem to be stuck in the past. Still, I promise you it'll be a good night!"

I smile and try to ignore the sense of dread that has been growing in the pit of my stomach since our last phone call. James is being really friendly and acting just like his usual self, and I'm starting to wonder whether I read too much into his last letter. It's probably me. Even though I'm feeling a bit better, it's naive to assume that I'm the old Ella. It's going to take a while before I can trust my own judgement again.

"Are Beth and Paul meeting us there?" I ask.

"Yeah. Said we'd be there about seven, and it looks like we'll be bang on time," James says as he pulls into the car park just down the road from the pub. "Ready to see what a Sunday night in Whitby has to offer?"

"Ready," I reply.

I let James take my hand as we walk the short distance to the Stag's Head. As we draw close, the noise surprises me, and I feel myself tense up. James notices and squeezes my hand.

"We don't have to go in there," he says, stopping walking. "If it's too much, I understand. It sounds like the football crowd is still in there from earlier, and it can be a bit rowdy until they leave."

I look up at him, and our eyes lock on each other. His gaze is intense, and I can feel the sincerity and warmth radiating from him. My insides quiver as I weigh up my options. I don't want to let him down. I force a smile onto my face, take a deep breath to steady my nerves, and force my fears away. "Let's go win this quiz," I say in as confident a voice as I can muster.

We step into the pub, the smell of beer and whisky wafting in the air. I feel my heart racing as we approach the bar, and James begins conversing with the bartender.

"What do you fancy?" he asks me gently, and I look up at the selection of drinks on offer.

I haven't had anything stronger than a cup of coffee since I moved here, but the idea of a glass of red to steady my nerves is too much to resist.

"A merlot would be great," I say and go to get some money out of my purse.

"One glass of merlot and one cranberry J2O," James says to the bartender. "And these drinks are on me," he adds.

"Are you not drinking?" I ask him, wondering if I should have stuck with soft drinks too.

"Driving," James reminds me, shaking his keys.

Shit, I could have got a taxi if it was going to be a problem.

"Sorry," I mutter. "I didn't think."

James shakes his head and gives me a reassuring smile. "Don't worry, Ella. You're here to enjoy yourself tonight, and I am here to ensure that happens. Look, Beth's over there. Let's go and join her, and I can introduce you properly before the quiz starts."

I nod in agreement as James takes the drinks from the barman and passes me mine. He smiles at me reassuringly and guides me away from the noise of the bar to the quiet table near the window where Beth is sitting.

"Ella!" Beth shouts as we get close. "I've been looking forward to meeting you since Paul said you'd be coming. And James! How are you feeling now? Good? I've been asking Paul to check on you, but it's so much better to see you for myself."

I have no idea what she's talking about. Has James been ill? This is starting to feel awkward already. I smile and take a seat, trying to stay calm and act normal.

"I'm fine, Beth," James replies, pushing her off him. "Where's Paul?"

"Oh, just over there talking to some bloke at the bar like usual," Beth replies. "I'm sure he'll be over soon."

I look around, trying to see if I can spot him, and it doesn't take long. He seems to be laughing at a joke somebody is telling him, completely lost in conversation.

"So, Ella," Beth says, looking at me kindly. "Tell me about you! I want to know everything!"

I gulp a mouthful of my wine and feel it warm me up, as well as give me an excuse not to speak for a few seconds.

"Well," I say slowly, trying to think of something to say. "I moved here a couple of weeks ago on a complete whim."

"Nice!" Beth says. "The cottage on the way to Staithes, yeah?"

"Yeah," I reply. "How did you know that?"

Beth laughs and looks at James, who looks embarrassed and continues to glance over my shoulder at Paul, waiting for him to come over. "James tells Paul everything, and then I convince Paul to tell me all his secrets. Small town - not much goes on here."

I look at James then and see his discomfort, which makes me smile. It's nice to know that he feels as awkward as I do.

"But you didn't tell me about yourself!" Beth laughs, turning back to me. "What does Ella do?"

Beth's eyes are locked onto mine, and she looks genuinely interested. I wonder what she'll think of me if I tell the truth.

"Well, I'm an author," I say, again feeling awkward as I say those words out loud.

"No way? What books do you write? Will I have read them?"

"Not unless you read historical romance," I say.

"Oh no, no, wait. Don't tell me you're Ella Park?"

"Um-"

"Author of Passion and Petticoats?"

"That's me," I smile, shocked to meet someone outside of a book signing who's read my first novel.

"Oh. My. God!" Beth almost squeals. "Hey, Paul, come over here. You'll never guess who James is dating. Only the author of my favourite romance novel. The one I didn't shut up about for all of last year!"

"Are you really?" Paul asks, and I feel the heat rising to my cheeks as I blush. "Beth made me drive all the way to York for a book signing last March. I knew I recognised you when you came to the boat looking for James."

"Ok, you have to tell me everything," Beth says as she nudges James out of the way and sits beside me at the table. "Have you started writing the sequel yet? There's going to be a sequel, isn't there?"

I laugh. "Yes, there's going to be a sequel. But no, I haven't started writing it." I glance over to James, knowing he knows the full story, and he gives me a reassuring smile. "That's why I moved to Whitby," I continue. "To see if a break from the city could give me the inspiration I need to start."

"The Stag's Head Quiz will be starting in five minutes," I hear a voice rumbling over the microphone. "Make sure you have your phones turned off and your pencils and paper ready."

Beth waits for him to finish and then takes my hands in hers. "Ok, I just want to say that I am a massive fan, but I'm not going to totally freak out and be a weirdo right now. I'm so excited that you're here, though, and I can see us being great friends."

Her enthusiasm is infectious, and James was right; I do love her. She feels like the sister I never had, and apart from Jess, I don't have any close female friends. It's hard to explain, but you sometimes just know when someone amazing is in your life.

"I hope so," I reply in earnest. "I don't know anybody here apart from James and the guy on the market who I don't seem to be able to escape without buying all his aubergines."

Beth laughs long and hard. "Oh god, you don't mean Steve, do you? That man could sell fish to a fisherman. Just tell him no, or you'll have enough fruit and veg to open your own vegan restaurant before long. Ask me how I know?"

"How do you know?" I ask, taking the bait.

"Because I fell for the same spiel and now have to have carrot cake specials on the menu nearly every day," she laughs. "There's honestly no escaping him. So, tell me more about your career. How do you even get started with something like writing?"

"Come and sit back round here, babe," Paul encourages Beth. "James has invited Ella out tonight, and I'm sure he wants to be the one to sit next to her."

"Shhh," Beth shrugs him off, but she does move to stand up so James can retake his seat. "Ella was just telling me about how she does her author thing."

"Sorry," he whispers. "She can be a bit full on."

"Don't apologise," I smile. "I really like her."

"So, how do you do your author thing?" Paul asks.

I look at James and see him giving Paul the look that means to shut up, but he doesn't have to. I don't mind sharing my secret now. I squeeze James' hand in reassurance and let them know the real reason why I moved here.

"Shiiiiiiiiiiiit," Beth says, her eyes wide. This girl really does wear her heart on her sleeve.

"Yeah," I say, slightly concerned that I've totally just stunted the conversation.

"Did you know about this, mate?" Paul asks James, and he nods, squeezing my hand back under the table.

"It's ok," I say, trying to deflect from the seriousness of it all. "Things are getting better, and I'm hopeful I'll be able to start writing again soon."

"Oh, you have to," Ella begs me. "Doesn't she Paul?"

"I don't think she'll shut up until you do," Paul laughs. "But seriously, if you ever think anyone is watching you or that you're in danger, you give one of us a call, yeah? We'll make sure you're ok."

"Yes," Beth says instantly. "Give me your number, and I'll text you mine and Paul's so you have them all."

I pass my phone over to her and let her do her thing, again feeling truly happy to have been welcomed so quickly into their group.

16

JAMES

I can't keep my eyes off Ella as she tells Beth and Paul her story. I can see the pain on her face and would do almost anything to take it away. No one should have to live through what she has.

I've been struggling with that damn pain in my abdomen since we first arrived here, my stomach churning like a wrung-out washcloth. I press my hand into my side, gritting my teeth as I try to suppress the pulsing ache; Beth and Paul are thankfully too engrossed in Ella to notice my distress. At least I have my follow-up doctor's appointment tomorrow, so I should get some answers.

I smile at Ella as she looks over to me, squeezing her with my free hand again to show her that I'm here for her. She had seemed so timid when I picked her up from her cottage, but Beth's enthusiasm is contagious, and it's great to see her blossoming into a much more confident version of herself around my friends. She looks as comfortable and content as could be as part of our circle.

"Right, are we ready to actually win this quiz tonight?" Paul asks, looking at Ella with a grin on his face. "James tells me you're our secret ingredient to success, Ella, so I have high hopes."

Ella laughs, and I smile as I see a blush creep up her cheeks. "Oh god, I hope I can live up to my reputation."

The quiz starts, and I find myself distracted again, my eyes wandering around the pub as I try to focus on quashing the pain in my stomach. The girls from last week are here, chatting animatedly at the bar, and the guy we took out on the fishing boat earlier today sits not that far from them. He looks at me and gives me a stilted smile which I return half-heartedly.

"You should know this one, mate," Paul says, distracting me back to the table.

"Huh?"

"Who has been Sonic the Hedgehog's rival since 2001?"

Ella looks at me hopefully as I dig into my brain for gaming trivia.

"Shadow," I say, and Paul high-fives me dramatically across the table.

"Knew you'd get it," he says.

I look down at the sheet and notice we've got an answer for every question so far. Makes a change.

"Here, why don't you write for a bit?" Beth says, pushing the paper over to me. "I'm off to the bar for another drink. Anyone else want one?"

"I'd love another glass of red," Ella replies, standing up. "Here, I'll come with you."

I watch as Ella and Beth head to the bar, Ella's long skirt drifting gracefully behind her.

"Looks like you've finally found yourself a perfect girl, mate," Paul says, winking at me.

"She's great, isn't she?" I reply.

"And she obviously likes you too. I can tell by the way she looks at you."

I smile and nod, feeling a warmth radiating from the centre of my body.

"She's got a lot going on at the moment," I say, watching Ella as she twists her fingers nervously at the bar. "But she's worth it. Thanks for making her feel so comfortable."

"Well, I wasn't exactly gonna list all the bad things from your past, was I?" Paul laughs loudly, making Beth and Ella turn around.

"Hey! You make me sound like a right bad boy," I say, yet I can't help but smile.

The rest of the evening unfolds as if in a dream. Ella takes small, joyful sips of red wine, and I casually grit my teeth against the dull ache that radiates from my side with every movement. Before I know it, the quiz is over, and Ella's stepped up to hand our quiz sheet in.

"I've got high hopes for tonight," I tell her once she returns. "I really do think you might have helped Fisherman's Friends achieve a win!"

"We'll see." Ella's lips turn into an uneasy smile as she sits down beside me. Beth and Paul chatter away on the other side of the table, seemingly oblivious to the tension radiating from Ella. My side aches, and I can't help but worry - maybe it's not just physical pain I'm feeling right now. I try to ignore it, but it's clear there's more going on with Ella than a smile can hide.

Beth and Paul start talking to Ella again, and I watch them as though in a trance. She's smiling at them and taking part, but her smile doesn't reach her eyes. Between the pain and an unhappy date, I'm about ready for this night to be over.

"And we have our winners," Graham's voice comes loud over the microphone. "It's a two-way tie on 39 points between Lonely Leonard and Fishermen's Friends. If you want to make your way to the bar, a drink on the house is waiting for you."

"Yes, Ella," Beth shouts. "I knew you could do it! You have to be part of our quiz team every Sunday from now on. What do you say?"

"Sure," Ella replies. "I'd love that."

"So, what drink would you like? I'll go and order them."

I glance at Ella and notice her eyes darting around the room, her lips pressed into a thin line. I can tell she wants to be anywhere else but here, but she smiles politely and asks for another glass of red. I know she's trying to hide how she's feeling, but I can see it in her eyes; the tightness in her jaw, the way her knuckles turn white as she grips the stem of the glass Beth passes her.

"You've definitely got to go home and write that book," Beth encourages Ella as she sits back down at the table. "If you need anyone to bounce ideas off, I'm only a phone call away."

"I think I might," Ella replies. "Or, at the very least, I'll open my laptop and try writing an outline."

Thirty minutes later, we're all saying our goodbyes. I quickly remind Paul that I'll be late to work in the morning, and Beth leans in to give me a hug, whispering "she's a keeper," in my ear. I really hope she's right, but I have a feeling she isn't.

I lace my fingers with Ella's and lead her out of the pub, saying goodnight to a few of my fishing mates on the way out. A heavy silence settles between us as we make the short walk back to my car. Her eyes, slightly glazed from the wine, are almost droopy from exhaustion, and I can tell she's eager to get home.

"So, did you enjoy your first night out in Whitby?" I say as we get back into the car, and I prepare to reverse.

"Yeah, it was fun," Ella replies.

I glance at her sideways and can see she's struggling and wish she would just be open and honest with me like she was the other night at her cottage.

"Beth seems to really like you, eh?" I say, wanting to make conversation, hoping it will put her at ease. "I knew she would, but it's crazy that you're the same author she didn't shut up about for most of last year."

"Yeah. Small world," Ella replies.

I can't help but notice how short and clipped she's being now that we're alone together, and honestly, it's frustrating as hell.

"Do you think you'll go back to writing?" I ask.

"Yeah. I'm going to give it a try when I get back," she says, her eyes looking at anybody but me.

We make the rest of the short drive in silence, and as I pull up to her cottage, I've had enough of trying to get something, anything, out of her.

"Ella, is there something wrong?" I say as I turn the ignition off and look her directly in the eyes. She seems wary, afraid, and I have no clue what I could have done to make her feel this way.

"No, I'm fine," she says, picking up her purse and preparing to open the door. "Thank you for a lovely night."

"Ella," I repeat, grabbing her wrist to stop her from leaving. "Please. Just tell me what I've done wrong."

"It's nothing, James. Just leave it, ok?"

Before I can reply, she pulls away, jumps out of the car, and walks quickly to her door. I want to follow her, to make her open up and tell me what's wrong, but all I can do is sit there as my heart sinks and watch her disappear into the darkness.

My knuckles turn white as I clench the steering wheel in frustration, tears stinging my eyes. A sharp pain pierces my stomach, and I double over, feeling like I'm going to be sick. Ella has a way of making my thoughts spin out of control, and no matter how much I try to convince myself that she's worth it, I have to admit that the constant hot and cold is becoming too much for me to deal with. Every moment with her is starting to cause me pain, and I can't keep spending every waking moment wondering what is going on with her. With us. If there even is an us.

I flick the key in the ignition and feel the engine rumble to life. I drive away from Ella's cottage, not looking back, and weave my way through winding coastal roads before arriving at a secluded viewpoint where I park. I desperately need some quiet and some time to think.

I step out of the car and inhale the salty air while leaning against my bonnet. The sky is beginning to clear, and the stars are twinkling like diamonds against a navy-blue backdrop. The waves sparkle in the starlight, and I feel a sense of peace washing over me. I wonder if my dad is up there, looking down on me. *If you're there, Dad, please tell me what you would do.*

I watch the waves roll in, one after another, like a soothing rhythm that always remains the same. Sometimes the waves are calm, caressing the shoreline like a gentle touch; other times, they are vicious and angry, pounding against the rocks and spewing white spray into the air. It reminds me of relationships, how everything can be perfect one minute but then wildly out of control the next. But if you find someone who could make all those amazing moments last, the pain of the bad times would be worth it.

Ignoring the dull ache in my side that is trying to tell me otherwise, I know I need to speak to Ella. I can't keep living like this. I need to talk to her, tell her exactly how I feel and what's going on in my head. Our relationship might be new, but with how emotional we've been with each other in such a short space of time, the connection between us feels like that of two people who have known each other for a lifetime. And taking this step is the only way I'll be able to move forward one way or the other.

My throat is dry, and my palms are sweaty as I open my car door and grab my phone. I open my messaging app and try to think what to write. Should I tell her I'm coming over now? Should I write everything down in a message? My fingers hover mid-air as the screen goes black, a call notification taking precedence.

Ella's name appears on the caller ID, and I find my heart racing even more than before. I answer without hesitation.

"James?" Ella's voice sounds strained, barely a whisper as she speaks my name.

Fear seizes me in its icy clutches as I scramble back into my car. "Ella? What is it? Are you ok?"

"James. I need you."

The line goes dead. I turn the ignition and drive as quickly as I can towards her home.

17

ELLA

I hang up the phone and slouch back against the door. Tears fall from my eyes, and it's taking every bit of effort I have not to walk out into the night and never return. James is the only person close enough to me to help me right now. I had to call him even if I don't particularly want to see him.

I wait for what feels like an eternity before I hear his car rumbling back up my drive. I hear the car door open and shut with a loud bang, followed by the sound of his footsteps running along the path to my cottage.

"Ella! Ella! Are you in there? Are you ok?"

He tries the door handle, but I've bolted it tight. I force myself into a standing position and open it, letting him in.

The second he sees me, he rushes towards me and takes me in his arms. Those strong warm arms that offer me so much comfort. I need this right now. I need him.

James keeps hold of me while pushing the door closed behind him and bolting the lock. I want to fall back to the floor, my breathing still stilted, but he holds me up, keeps me standing.

"Ella, what's happened? You need to tell me."

I can't find my voice, so instead, I just let out a few more sobs and collapse into his embrace. He holds me close and whispers words of comfort into my ear, stroking my hair gently. His tenderness almost makes me cry even more.

He takes me by the arm, and I feel a warmth spread through my body despite the chill of the night. He tucks me into the soft embrace of the sofa and gently lays my dressing gown over my shoulders. A moment later, he disappears into the kitchen, and I hear the low whistle of the teapot coming to life.

What is wrong with me? I am trying so hard to hold it together, but I think it's time to admit that I'm a mess, and nothing is going to change.

James returns a few minutes later with two steaming mugs of tea in his hands. I take mine gratefully and try to force a smile. He sits down next to me on the sofa, so close that I can feel the heat radiating from his body, and I'm instantly reminded of the last time he was here, of how I had opened up to him and bared my soul.

I let him take one of my hands and look into his eyes. They look sad, filled with a deep compassion that almost makes me cry. I squeeze his hand, letting him know this isn't his fault. It's mine.

"Please, Ella," James says, almost pleading. "You have to tell me what's going on."

"I don't know how," I say. There's so much stuff going through my head right now that I'm struggling to make sense of it all myself. I just know I don't want to be alone right now.

"Can you try?" he asks, and I know I need to give him something.

I reach to the side of the sofa and pick up my laptop. I slowly open the screen and enter my password before passing it to him. I don't need to use words to show him how bad everything has got.

I watch James' face as he looks through my laptop and sees the hundreds of notifications constantly pouring in.

"Read them," I tell him. "Go ahead."

James' eyes are wide as he uses the trackpad on my laptop to open my email account and reads a few of the more recent emails.

"You can check my social media too if you like - he's everywhere."

"Jesus," James replies, pushing a hand through his thick dark hair. "Did you-"

"I walked through the door and felt like maybe I did have it in me to start drafting my second novel," I say through exaggerated sobs. "I pulled my laptop out of my suitcase and turned it on. Within seconds of it booting, I was a wreck. I'm sorry I called you back here after being so rude when you dropped me off. I just panicked and didn't know what to do."

I take a sip of the milky tea James' brought me and let the warmth spread through me. I let myself slide into the sofa and tuck my feet under myself. As ridiculous as it is, this feels like a cry for help, and I need someone to stay with me until I can think straight again.

"Oh, Ella," James murmurs, pulling me close. I rest my head against his shoulder, soaking in his comfort.

"What am I going to do?" I ask.

"That's not important right now," James replies. "You just need to rest."

"Are you sure you're ok with that?" I ask.

"What? Why wouldn't I be?" he replies, almost startled.

"Your second letter implied I was moving way too slow for you," I say, finally bringing it up. "And then the man at the bar in the pub told me that you were hosting sex parties on your fishing boat and-"

"What second letter?"

My hands shake as I pull the crinkled envelope from my dressing gown pocket and throw it at him. He picks it up and reads it, his face growing pale with worry.

"Ella. I didn't write this," he whispers. "And I haven't been doing anything of the sort on the boat either."

"That's not possible," I say. "I saw your handwriting in the pub tonight, and it matches both letters."

"It doesn't make sense," James replies, panic creeping into his voice. He runs his hand through his hair and slides off the sofa before pacing around the room.

"James?" I ask softly, watching him. "What is going on?"

"Fuck, Ella, I don't know." He sounds like he wants to say more, like he's thinking everything over in his head.

"At first, I thought it was me, that I was taking things the wrong way. And you seem so different in person. Sweet and genuine. But this letter," I pick it up and unfold it, my tears soaking the page, "this letter and the news about the boat made me think I don't know you at all."

James returns to the couch where I'm sitting and takes both of my hands in his while locking my gaze. "Ella, you have to believe me. I did not write that letter, and I can explain what happened on the boat today too."

I don't know what to think or what to believe, but the desperation in his voice is all I can focus on.

"Who else would have written it?" I whisper.

He looks at my laptop again and opens an email that just came in. His eyes are wide with fear, and it makes my heart feel like it's going to beat out of my chest.

"What is it?" I ask.

He passes me the laptop, and I read.

Break it off with him, Ella. He deserves better than you. If I see you with him again, I promise you it will be for the last time. This is your final warning.

Attached to the email is a photo of us leaving the pub together this evening.

"Probably the guy who wrote this," he says.

My insides churn as I feel my world spin out of control. My stomach threatens to release its contents, and I grab the sofa cushion, trying to calm the waves of nausea building up inside me. I can feel the panic building again, and I'm struggling to breathe. He has found me now. That much is clear.

"But how does he know your handwriting?" I ask, my voice trembling. James shakes his head, clearly as confused as I am.

"I think it's time we went to the police," he replies. His voice is firm but gentle, and I admit I think he's right.

I stand up and walk away from James, trying to regain composure as I try to get my head around everything that's happened. When I glance back over my shoulder, I see him hunched over my laptop, fingers flying across the keyboard as he quickly opens the North Yorkshire Police website with the online crime reporting page in full view.

"We can do it together," he says, holding out his arm for me to join him. I look at him and catch his eye just as I feel tears welling up behind mine.

"I'm sorry you've been caught up in this mess," I say, struggling to blink the tears away.

James places the laptop on the coffee table before approaching me near the window. He slowly wraps his arms around me, and I feel my body instinctively melt into his embrace. His warmth is comforting, and, despite the threats, I feel safe in his arms.

"You have nothing to apologise for, Ella," he says, kissing me softly on my forehead.

"I do," I reply. "I believed you'd written that second letter and I didn't even mention it to you. It was posted when Jess was here, and she seemed so sure it was from you that I didn't even question it."

James's eyes widen in disbelief, and his forehead creases as he looks down at me. "You don't think Jess could be behind all of this, do you?" His voice is shaky, and he absently runs a hand through his already dishevelled hair, his mind feverishly trying to make sense of it all.

"I don't see how she could be," I reply, my mind not wanting to go there. "She's been encouraging me to go to the police for months. She had no idea I'd moved here either at first. And she helped me loads last week."

"True," he replies, still working his hand through his hair. "Well, I think we need to get the police involved now. Whoever this man is, he's following you, and he's following me now as well. I will do whatever I can to keep you safe, Ella, but I think we need to let the professionals get involved. With the photographs and the letter, there may be something more that they can do."

"Ok," I say, my heart pounding. "I'm ready."

I take James' hand and let him lead me back to the sofa.

"I'll type the answers in," he says, "but we'll fill it out together."

I'm shaking as he types, but I know this is for the best. I feel the weight of every second tick by as James' fingers fly across the keyboard, filling the report in. Sweat beads on my forehead, and my fingers tremble as I read through it all and click "submit".

Thankfully James performs the arduous task of going through the seemingly endless emails and sorting out those that are the best for evidence. I'd thought Jess was monitoring my accounts, but maybe they'd become too much for her as well. Rather than get her involved again, James methodically downloads them and shows me the worst ones while sitting quietly by my side and lending his emotional support. I will never be able to thank him for everything.

A reference number flashes on the screen, and I blink hard, willing away the tears of relief.

"Do you want me to stay tonight," James asks as he closes my laptop and pulls me in for a warm embrace. "I can kip on the sofa if it will help to reassure you that you're safe."

"Thank you," I reply, the relief evident in my voice. "There's a spare bedroom, though; you don't have to sleep on the sofa. Trust me; it's really not comfortable."

James really has done more than anyone else to try and make sense of what's been happening, and I feel better knowing he's here with me, at least for a little while.

"What about tomorrow," he adds, "do you need me to stay with you in case the police get in touch?"

I shake my head. "No, that's ok. I know you have work, and I don't want to disrupt your life in the same way that I disrupted Jess'."

James kisses me on the forehead, and I go to bed feeling a sense of relief. I still don't feel safe, but I feel better knowing I'm not alone anymore.

"I promise you, Ella. One day, this will all be over. And you will write again."

18

JAMES

I walk to the harbour from the doctors feeling numb. Bowel cancer. Stage 2. "Age is on your side," Doctor Todd had told me, but I know how this is going to go. A 90% survival rate sounds good, but if my dad hadn't been able to overcome it, what were the chances I'd be able to?

I take my phone from my pocket and see I've had a missed call from Ella. I return it as I make the short walk to the fishing boat to meet Paul.

"Hey, Ella, how are you? Sorry I missed your call."

"I'm good," she replies, and I can almost hear her smiling through the phone. "I've just had a call from the police, actually, and they seem to be taking it seriously this time. I, um, well, I wondered if you'd like to come over this evening so I can fill you in? I can cook dinner for us if you'd like?"

"I'd love to," I reply, knowing there's nowhere else I'd rather be right now. Going back to my flat and dealing with this news alone is definitely not appealing, and I don't want to sit around Paul and Beth's either. I know Beth will fuss over me, and I need some space to get my head straight first.

"Okay, brilliant," Ella replies. "Do you want to come at about half 6? I'll get dinner ready for shortly after."

"Sure, I'll be there," I reply before hanging up.

I continue walking along the cobbled pavement towards the harbour and soon see Paul. He's already loaded the boat, and we're only a couple of hours behind our usual schedule.

I jump aboard, my movements feeling almost like I'm operating on autopilot and instantly start unwinding the rope that's securing the boat to the dock.

"How did it go?" Paul asks me as he stands behind the wheel, preparing to leave.

I don't know what to say to him. How the fuck do you tell your best mate you have cancer? I'm going to have to have this conversation with my mum too. She never got over losing my dad. I can't believe she's going to be faced with going through this all again.

I force back the tears that are threatening to fall and join him by the wheel. "Let's not talk about it right now, eh?" I say, wanting to have one last trip where nothing has changed.

Due to us leaving late, we decide not to head to our usual haunts and instead travel south to the spot where we took the tourists yesterday.

"What did you think of that guy Leonard?" I ask Paul as he slows the boat down. "I saw you talking to him at the bar."

"Aye, I thought he was alright," Paul replies. "He's having a shit time of it with his mum being ill, so just wanted to extend the hand of friendship, you know?"

"Yeah," I say, not entirely convinced. "He told Ella we were selling tourist sex parties when she went to hand the quiz sheet in."

"Ha, imagine if we were," Paul laughs. "Would probably be able to make enough money to afford Beth's wedding plans if that was true. He did ask about you, though."

I wonder if I'm overthinking things. Paul seems to think he was just joking around.

"What did he want to know?"

"Oh, you know, just asking how you became a fisherman and how long you've lived around here. I totally bigged you up, mate, don't worry."

I laugh but can't help feeling a bit uneasy. I try to remember whether he looked like the man who'd made Ella uncomfortable at the book cafe, but I can't be sure. I'm starting to get the feeling that there's more to him than meets the eye.

I pick up some bait and begin loading my reels, needing to focus on the task at hand and wash my mind clear of the cancer news. It works. Ashore, my mind is in overdrive, but as soon as I'm on the boat, I feel at peace.

"I told the head chef at The Ivy that we'd try and catch them 40 seabass for their special tonight," Paul says as he loads his reels and throws them out over the side of the boat. "If we manage it, we'll get paid as much as we would for our usual mackerel catch."

"Sounds good," I reply.

"So, want to tell me what Todd said?"

Paul joins me in sitting down as we wait for our reels to hopefully attract some big bass. I can see the concern on his face, and though I really don't want to talk about this right now, I can see I'm going to have to.

"Cancer," I reply. "Stage 2."

"Holy shit, man," Paul exclaims, jumping up and crushing me in his arms. "Why didn't you say? What the fuck are you doing working straight after news like that?"

Paul pushes his hands through his hair, clearly distraught, and I find I have no words of wisdom to help. I have no clue what to do either.

We both sit in silence for a moment, no words able to pass between us. I look out over the sea, the tainted water and the blackening sky reminding me of the dark road ahead. Still, a storm is good. A storm would give me something to focus on that isn't this disease running through my body.

Seconds later, big fat raindrops begin to fall from the sky. I listen to the sound of it pitter-pattering against the boat's hull, a sense of calm rushing over me. I'm getting soaked, but I don't care.

"Fucking hell," Paul exclaims, pulling up his hood. "We're not gonna be able to catch much in this. Come on, let's get home."

But I don't move. I sit immovable on the wet boat watching the sheets of rain sweeping over the sea. I've caught bass in the rain before, it can be done, and I don't feel like being comfortable and warm at home right now.

"James," Paul encourages me. "Come on, let's get the lines in and head back."

I wish I could tell him to go back on his own. Leave me to it. My skin shivers from the cold and my fingers turn red, but I don't want to leave.

Paul huffs in exasperation but comes and sits back next to me. "We're doing this then?" he asks.

"You need the money for your wedding," I reply.

THE SUN HAS STILL NOT MANAGED to break through the clouds by the time we arrive back at Whitby Harbour three hours later. The sea is a deep indigo, the sky a cloudy grey, but our boat is heavy with an array of seabass, all ready for the posh hotel in town.

My face feels blistered from the icy winds that had picked up halfway through our journey, and I clench my numb fingers around the wheel of the boat as we pull in to dock. I appreciated Paul staying with me and letting me finish this job. It was probably going to be my last one for a while.

"Do you want to come back to mine after we drop this off?" Paul asks as we finish loading up our catch. "You can stay for dinner if you like. We'll get a takeaway."

"Nah, thanks though, mate," I reply. "I told Ella I'd head to hers. She's cooking."

"Does she know?" Paul asks.

"You're the only person I've told so far. I'm going to break it to her tonight; I just need to think of the right words."

Paul places his hand on my shoulder in comfort, and I can't help but think of how much I will miss him if I don't make it through this.

"They can treat it, though? Right?" Paul pushes as I don't answer.

"I hope so, mate. Todd said something about chemo. I was struggling to focus on the details after the news. He also mentioned having some more tests to see if it's spread."

"Well, you make sure you go for them, you hear me?" Paul says, entirely focusing on me now rather than our catch. "Anything that they can do for you, just take it. Don't be a martyr, James. You have to beat this. Promise me you'll do everything you can to beat it."

Paul wipes his sleeve across his brow, brushing away the tears pooling in his eyes. The sound of rain thrums heavily against the ground, each drop like a hammer driving me further into despair.

"I promise," I say. "I'll do everything I can."

Paul nods, clinging to my words.

I stand at the bow of the boat and gaze upon the horizon, feeling my determination grow. I have weeks of treatment ahead of me, and I know it won't be easy, but I need to at least try. I have to. For her.

19

ELLA

After speaking to James, I made myself busy. I headed into town and bought some fresh veggies from Steve at the market before nipping to the butcher and purchasing a couple of rib-eye steaks. I'd just managed to get back to my car before thunder had rolled through the sky and the heavens had opened. Giant drops of rain pelted the cobbled streets with a ferociousness I'd never quite seen before. I thought about James and Paul out on the boat and hoped they'd managed to find shelter somewhere.

Upon returning to my cottage, I'd lit the fire in the living room and got to work preparing dinner. I planned to cook the steaks once James arrived, but I prepared the veggies and also set to work on my grand finale - a delicious honeycomb cheesecake. It had been years since I'd broken out my baking supplies, but I was proud of myself for making such a good-looking dessert.

James was worth it, I knew that much now, and I hoped he would enjoy it and accept my apology for how I'd treated him after our date last night.

After double-checking that I had nothing left to prepare, I set the table and got a couple of candles out for a centrepiece. Then, I drew a hot bath and poured in a few droplets of lavender oil. I slid into the steaming water and let the heat of it ease my muscles.

The rain continued to pour down outside, and I couldn't help but think how perfect this weather was for writing in. I used to love snuggling up on the sofa with my laptop and letting the words fall free. With the police now taking an interest in the case, and the support of my friends, maybe I really could get back to writing again.

Once the bath water cools, I force myself to get out and get dressed. I pull on a pair of high-waisted jeans and a soft, cream-coloured cashmere sweater, enjoying the feel of it against my skin. I dry my hair and tie it back in a low bun before applying some light makeup. A glance at the clock tells me that James will be here soon, and I'm nervous with excitement. I really want to make a good impression on him tonight. Show him that the real Ella can be nice to spend time with.

The rumble of a car engine makes me peek out of the window, and I watch as James pulls up. He stays seated for a minute or two before getting out of his car, and I wonder if he's as anxious as I am. I rush to the door, not waiting for him to knock and open it wide.

"Hello you," he says as he sees me, a big smile on his face. "I bought you some flowers." He's holding a large bouquet, and a blush creeps up my cheeks as I accept them.

"Thank you," I reply. "That's so kind of you. Come on in out of the rain. I've lit the fire, so it's all warm and cosy in here."

James follows me inside and kicks his shoes off near the front door. I close it behind him and take his coat before finding a vase for my lovely flowers and placing them on the fireplace in the centre of the room. They're absolutely gorgeous, their brightness providing a fantastic contrast to the dark stormy weather.

"Do you want to join me in the kitchen?" I ask as he stands awkwardly near the door. "It won't take me long to cook this up. I hope you like steak?"

"Love it," he smiles. He sits on one of the breakfast chairs that line my counter and watches me cook.

"Let me guess, medium rare?"

"Medium," he replies. "If that's ok."

"Of course. Would you like a drink while you wait? I've got a bottle of wine, or there's orange juice, lemonade-"

"Just a water would be great, thanks."

I hand James a glass of ice-cold water and start cooking our dinner. It doesn't take me long, thanks to all the preparation I did earlier and by the time the sun begins to fall beneath the horizon, I've dished up the food onto our plates. I carry them through to the small dining table and quickly light the candles I'd placed there earlier.

"Tuck in," I say while watching him eagerly, hoping it tastes good.

"This tastes amazing," James says as he takes a bite of his steak. "You are seriously the best cook ever."

"Are you comparing my steak to frozen ready meals?" I laugh. "Because I'll still take the compliment even if you are."

"I do tend to live off Pot Noodles and takeaways," he admits. "But seriously, this is delicious."

"I'm glad you like it," I say. "And I'm super happy you could come over this evening."

I munch on a stalk of asparagus, fully relaxing in my surroundings. Despite my misgivings about James since I got here, it's nice to be enjoying dinner with someone that I know cares about me - someone I can trust to assist me during a difficult time.

"Speaking of which, I wanted to apologise for last night," I say. "I shouldn't have just taken the word of some crazy man at the bar, and I should have asked you about the letter when I'd first received it. But more than that, you've been nothing but kind to me, and I had no right to push you away due to my messed-up view of the world."

"You've had a really tough time of it, Ella," he smiles, though I sense there's pain there too. "I honestly have only ever wanted what's best for you."

"I know," I reply, relishing his honesty. "I can see that now. I really am sorry for taking so long to realise it."

James smiles at me and takes hold of my hand across the table. "So, what did the police say? They phoned you, right?"

"Yeah, first thing. The policewoman I spoke to said that I have a case for harassment and malicious communications and that the email he sent with photographs could also lead to a charge for stalking. But the main issue is that they don't have any real leads to help them find out who's doing this. I said I'd take my laptop down to the police station tomorrow so they can do a forensic exam or whatever it is they do. They can keep hold of it too - stops me needing to read all of the emails he sends."

"That's great news," James replies, and I can tell he's genuinely pleased that something is going to be done about it. "I wonder if there's any CCTV that overlooks the pub too. If there is, you'd think they'd be able to narrow their list of suspects."

"I hadn't thought of that, but that's a good point! It sounds like my stalker might have actually messed up and revealed who he is."

I feel relieved at the prospect that this could be over very quickly.

"Have you heard from Jess at all?" James asks. "I thought she would be monitoring your phone once she returned to York. The police will probably want to look at that too."

"I haven't, actually," I say. "She's probably been busy catching up on everything after taking a week off, and to be honest, I haven't reached out to her either. I'll give her a call tomorrow and let her know what's been going on. I could probably take a road trip to York this weekend and get my phone back from her."

"I think that's a good idea," James replies. "She'd want to know, and she'd be pleased to know you've gone to the police, I think."

I clear our dinner plates away and prepare to serve the dessert I made earlier. "I hope you've got a bit of room left," I shout to James from the kitchen.

"Why?" he asks, almost suspiciously.

I walk back to the dining table carrying my piece de resistance, the cheesecake to rule all cheesecakes, a dessert sent from the heavens above for the man with the sweetest tooth I know.

"Oh wow," James exclaims as I place it on the table before us. "Don't tell me you made this?"

"Uh-huh," I say, a wide grin spreading across my face. "I made this for you as part of my apology. I had to guess what you'd like, but I know you love those caramel frappes from Beth's, so I assumed a honeycomb cheesecake would be a good bet."

James is silent for a moment, his eyes wide and his mouth agape, and I half wonder whether I've made a bad decision. Then, without saying a word, he stands up from his chair and pulls me close, pressing his lips to mine. His mouth is warm, and I feel tiny sparks of electricity on my skin as I melt into the kiss.

"You really like cheesecake, then?" I laugh as we break apart.

"I really like you," he says.

I can't help but feel like he has more to say, but as he opens his mouth to speak, his phone rings, interrupting the moment. He glances down at it and sends it to voicemail.

"Sorry," he mutters. He goes to put his phone back in his pocket, but it rings again.

"Answer it if you need to," I say. "The cheesecake can wait."

I cut us a slice each and take the remainder back into the kitchen while James answers his call.

"Sorry, that was Beth," he says, poking his head into the kitchen a couple of minutes later. "I've actually got some news of my own to share. I hoped to wait until after we'd finished eating, but I feel like I should tell you now."

"Go on," I say, moving around the countertop so that I'm standing next to him.

"I'm not quite sure how to say this," he starts. He has a pained look on his face, and I can tell it's not something good.

"Do you want to sit down?" I ask, and he nods.

I slip my fingers through his and lead him back into the front room, past the small dining table and towards the sofas. We sit down next to each other, and I take his hand in mine, squeezing it gently.

"You can tell me anything," I say, gazing up into his face. He smiles, but it doesn't reach his eyes, and I can tell something is wrong. Really wrong. "Is there something wrong with Beth? Or Paul?"

"No, it's me," he says, squeezing my hand for reassurance. "I went to the hospital last week for some tests, and, well, it's cancer."

"Shit, shit, shit," I say, not really knowing what to say. "Oh, James, why didn't you tell me? You've been so kind listening to my drama, and I had no idea what you'd been going through. I'm so sorry. I guess Beth knows? That's why she phoned? Do you want to go and see her? I can drive you if you do."

I'm speaking a thousand miles a minute, but I don't know what to do, what to think. Fuck, this is all such a mess. What is wrong with the universe?

"I only got the results this morning," James says, his voice trembling. "I told Paul this afternoon, and he tells Beth everything so..."

I take him in my arms and let him rest his head on my shoulder. "I'm so sorry," I mutter, hating myself for how inadequate that sounds. "If there's anything I can do, just let me know, ok? Anything at all."

"If we could stay in this moment forever, I'll die a happy man."

James squeezes me tight, and I hold him close, stroking my hands softly through his hair. While we're like this, we're in our own little bubble of safety and happiness. Nothing can break us apart.

"You're going to be ok," I murmur. "We're going to figure something out."

"I wish I'd met you when I was younger," James whispers. "Before everything that happened to you and before my diagnosis. I have a feeling we'd have had some really happy years together."

"You can't talk like that," I say. "We have all the time in the world."

I pull back from the embrace and look James in the eyes, wanting him to know that I truly believe the words I'm saying. People get awful diagnoses like this all the time, and they're ok. James will be ok too. He has to be.

I push my hands through his hair again and lean in to kiss him. I want nothing more than to feel his body pressed against mine tonight and to fall to sleep wrapped in his arms.

"You're staying here tonight," I tell him, and I'm not taking no for an answer.

"Are you sure?" he asks.

I don't answer with words. I kiss him again, taking my time as our lips connect. The kiss starts off tender but becomes more forceful as our passion grows. James pulls me close, pressing his body against mine and running his hands over my body.

"I'm sure," I whisper into his ear as he kisses my neck. "I can't bear to be without you right now."

I hold James' hand and lead him into my bedroom, closing the door softly behind us. It's time to show him exactly how much he means to me and how much I want him to live.

20

JAMES

I wake up in a haze of blissfulness as I breathe in the sweet aroma of Ella lying beside me. The world outside seems distant while I lay here, and I can almost pretend that everything that happened yesterday was nothing more than a bad dream. The storm had raged ferociously through the night, but I can feel the warmth of the sun's rays against my skin as they force their way through Ella's bedroom curtains.

I roll onto my side to look at Ella, marvelling at her beauty, and for a few moments, my trepidation about the future feels a million miles away. I remain there for as long as I can, looking at the gorgeous woman asleep beside me and basking in the newfound calm, knowing full well that soon enough, we'll have to confront the issues that plague us. But for now, I just want time to stop still and live in this moment forever.

After making love last night, we lay together in the darkness, limbs intertwined, for what felt like hours. The warmth of her body had soothed me, and I felt a contentment that had been missing in my life for so long, her presence like a blanket shielding me from the outside world. I never wanted it to end.

Ella's breathing eventually moves out of its steady rhythm,

breaking me out of my fantasy, and I look down at her as she opens her eyes.

"Morning, beautiful."

"Hello, gorgeous."

I take her in my arms and plant a kiss on her lips before returning my cheek to the nook of her neck while she wraps her arms around me.

"What time is it?"

"I have no idea. I think it's still early."

"Mmm, I could just stay here all day."

"Me too."

"Maybe we can come back here tonight and make the most of this bed," she says with a mischievous smile.

"I like the sound of that," I reply before kissing her again.

I'm broken away from the bliss by the sound of my phone ringing. I wait for a second or two to see if whoever's calling will hang up, but they don't, so I pull on my jeans and kiss Ella on the head before walking into the front room to answer it.

"Yes, this is he. Yes, no problem." I look down at my watch. "Ok, yes, I can be there. Thank you."

"Leaving already?" Ella asks as she joins me in the front room, yawning, with just a dressing gown tied around her. Gosh, she's beautiful.

"Yeah, the hospital has had a cancellation, so I get to go and have some more tests done. Lucky me."

"Do you want me to come with you?" she asks, her face full of sympathy that, while kind, makes me feel all kinds of shit after the lovely night we just had together.

"No, that's okay. It'll just be a lot of sitting around, and you have more important things to do. You've got to take your laptop down to the police station and call Jess and find out about your phone. Seriously, Ella, those things are important too!"

"That stuff can wait, James. Honestly, I can come with you if you'd like me to. It can't be easy going to all of these appointments alone."

Her face is sad, and I can tell she'd drop everything in seconds to be by my side throughout this. But I almost feel like I need to do it on my own. Right now, anyway.

I take her in my arms as she draws closer to me and hold her tight. "I'll be ok, Ella. If the offer's still there for a repeat of last night, though, you can count me in."

"Of course. You still have three-quarters of a gigantic cheesecake to get through!" She laughs, and I can't help but join in.

I finish getting dressed and pull my shoes and coat back on before drawing Ella in for one last kiss near the front door.

"Let me know how it goes," she says. "Good or bad, I'll keep my phone with me all day."

"I promise," I say, forcing a smile onto my face.

As I make my way to the car, I feel a pang of anxiety creeping up on me. I'm fully expecting these tests to show that the cancer has spread. I try to shake off the nerves and focus on the present. After all, I have a beautiful woman waiting for me, and I'm determined to enjoy every moment we still have together.

When I arrive at the hospital, I'm greeted by the usual sterile smell and the hustle and bustle of doctors and nurses going about their day. I check in at the desk, and the receptionist directs me to a waiting room. It's on the other side of the hospital from the one I was led to before, yet it almost looks identical. I don't know if it's meant to be soothing, but I can't help but think how depressing it is.

The sterile smell of the disinfectant and the sounds of beeping machines only make my anxiety worse. I try to distract myself by reading the text messages Beth had sent me overnight, but they just make me feel like I've got a death sentence. I know she means well, but it's too much.

"Mr Clarke?" I look up at the sound of my name. "If you'd like to come this way, please."

I follow an elderly-looking nurse through to a room where a machine that looks like a giant metal doughnut is waiting for me. I look at it ominously, not exactly looking forward to this.

"Ok, so we're going to give you a CT scan today, Mr Clarke. That will help to give us a better idea of how things are progressing."

I don't reply, not knowing what to say, so the nurse continues.

"If you'd like to undress and put this hospital gown on, the technician will be along shortly. Please make sure to remove any jewellery as well."

I nod and watch as she leaves the room before closing the door behind me. A few minutes later, I'm wearing an awful gown, and I've been strapped down to the scanner table. It feels claustrophobic, and I have to really focus on my breathing so as not to panic.

The technician's voice is steady and reassuring as he explains what I can expect to experience during the test. I try my best to stop panicking and focus so we can get this over with as quickly as possible. I can hold my breath when he tells me to. It won't be difficult.

A minute later and he's left the room, his voice now coming through the intercom. The machine whirrs and clicks as it moves me through slowly, and I hold my breath every time I'm instructed to.

As the CT scan continues, my mind starts to wander, and I again begin to breathe on autopilot. I think about my dad and how I got here, lying on a table, waiting for medical professionals to tell me exactly how bad things are. I think about everything I've taken for granted in life - my health, my loved ones, my job. And most of all, I think about Ella, the most beautiful girl I've ever met and how even that relationship is likely doomed before it's even really begun.

The machine gives a slight shudder, bringing me back to reality, and then there's silence before the technician's voice returns over the intercom. "The scan is complete. You can get dressed now." My muscles release their tension, and I sit up, undoing the straps that had held me in place and feeling the cool air hit my skin. Relief washes over me as I step off the table, grab my clothes and get dressed.

Once I'm ready, I follow the nurse into a smaller room for more blood tests before making my way back to the waiting room. I try not to think about how much my life is going to change. Instead, I focus on the present moment and the small things that bring me joy - the sound of the seagulls swarming around the harbour, the warmth of the sun on my skin, the beautiful girl waiting for me back at her house, caramel frappes and homemade cheesecake.

I wait for what feels like hours until, eventually, I hear my name being called. The same elderly nurse as before leads me down the hallway and into a small, cramped room that overlooks the car park below. The doctor slowly looks up from his computer and clears his throat while motioning for me to sit down. His voice is low, and I know what's coming.

I'm wrong.

The doctor's words send a chill through me as he speaks, but it's not the news I'd been expecting. I have a type of cancer called Non-Hodgkin's Lymphoma. It's a form of blood cancer, but it hasn't spread.

My heart pounds in my ears as he explains what's going to happen next, and despite it being better news than I'd expected, I'm still struggling to take it all in. I'm going to need to go through 18 weeks' worth of chemotherapy, but there's a good chance I'll make it through and enter recovery.

I force a composed smile and thank the doctor for his time. It's weird to act so calm at hearing news like that. You'd think you'd be sobbing and hysterical but no. A smile and a thank you, and I'm gone.

The taxi ride back to my house seems to go in slow motion. I blur out the words of the driver and the traffic around me and gaze out the window, looking up into the sky. It's a gorgeous spring day; you'd almost be forgiven for thinking summer was just around the corner. God, how I would love to experience just one more summer.

I turn my phone back on as I enter my flat for the first time in almost 24 hours. A cascade of notifications floods the screen, mainly from Beth, but there's also a missed call from Paul. Swallowing heavily, I take a deep breath and steel myself for what I need to do. They need to know.

I sit down on the sofa and press 'call'.

21

ELLA

I make myself a lovely warm cup of tea, carry it to the sofa, and press call. I've hardly spoken to Jess since she went back to the city, and I need to catch her up on everything that's been happening and ask if she minds me visiting her over the weekend. She answers on the second ring.

"Hey, you," I say, trying my best to sound optimistic. "I was worried I might have caught you at work. I'm not disturbing you, am I?"

"Oh no," Jess replies. "I'm in the office on my own today, actually, and you are saving me from extreme levels of boredom. So, what's up?"

"Well," where to begin? "There's a lot to catch you up on, but I'd rather do some of it in person. Are you free this weekend? I was thinking of coming back to the city for a night if you-"

"Oh no, not this weekend, honey, sorry. I've got a work thing that I can't get out of. End of the tax year, you know? Boss wants us all here."

"Isn't that in January?"

"Yeah, well, self-assessment is yeah, but we usually get all the self-employed people who want to send their returns off early contacting us, and Anna wants us to go through all the new tax rules and that. You know how it is?"

"Yeah," I mutter, disappointed to be blown off so quickly. "I understand. Can you post my phone back to me in that case?"

"Sure. Why?"

"Well, I guess I wanted to tell you this in person, but I finally reported the guy who's been harassing me to the police. I gave them my laptop yesterday, but they also want access to my phone so they can monitor what he's saying."

"Do they have any leads?" Jess asks me, her voice suddenly quiet.

"Not yet, I don't think. But if they can access my email and calls, they can track everything and make sure I'm safe. It saves you from having to do it. I know it can't have been easy."

"Oh ok, well that makes sense, I guess. Tell you what, why don't I see if I can get away early on Sunday, and I'll drive over to Whitby for the afternoon to see you? I can bring your phone with me then."

"That sounds great," I reply. "I have a lot to fill you in on. How is Anna, by the way? She wasn't mad at you for dropping everything for a week, was she?"

"No, honey, I told you, she was absolutely fine with it."

"Ok, well, as long as you're sure."

"I promise."

I hear what I think is a man's voice in the background but can't make out any words.

"Jess?"

"Shit, Ella, gotta go. My colleagues have come back early. See you Sunday."

She hangs up before I have a chance to reply.

I'm a bit lost on what to do now. I'd expected the call with Jess to last much longer, and James has gone to spend the day with Paul and Beth. The results of the scan he had yesterday had been semi-hopeful, but when Beth had phoned him this morning, pretty much pleading with him to go and see her, I'd encouraged it. He needed his friends right now. It was important to let them support him.

I write him a quick text: *Hope you're doing ok x* and look around the room wondering how I can pass the hours until I see him again.

My eyes settle on the teal moleskin notebook I purchased shortly after receiving my advance from my publisher. Its binder is soft to the touch, and I slowly trace the spine with my fingers and the corners of the pages with my thumbs, feeling a shiver run through me. I sit down and place the notebook on the coffee table before me, a blank canvas waiting to be filled.

I open it to the first page. The smell of fresh paper wafts through the air, a scent that takes me right back to my first year as a creative writing student in London. For the first time in months, I feel a stirring inside me—a sense of purpose, of urgency almost. I need to put words on the page and tell the world my story. I owe it to James to make it happen.

I pick up a biro and start writing. I don't think; I just let everything in my head spill out onto the page in fiction form. This isn't like me. I usually plan my stories for weeks before I begin writing, but not this time.

My slender fingers fly across the page, pounding out word after word, with a pen that feels like a magician's wand in my hand. Every half an hour, I pause to stretch my cramped arm and check in on James before continuing. By the time my stomach growls so much I'm forced to stop, I notice the sun sinking low in the sky, casting an orange-red hue on the world outside.

A text message from James startles me after the everlasting silence of the day. *Going to have a drink with Paul and Beth. Come and join us if you're free? x*

I'd love to, but I don't want to waste my inspiration while it's flowing so freely. This has only happened a couple of times before, and I don't want to stop, not even for an hour.

Not tonight. Writing. You have fun, though! x I quickly type back, and James replies just as quickly.

Writing? Yes! Go Ella! x

With a satisfied smile, I make myself a quick ham and cheese sandwich and grab a can of lemonade before shuffling back into the living room and flicking on a light. It illuminates the room with its warmth, and I can't help but reminisce about my childhood when I'd sit next to a small lamp and lose myself in writing about whole worlds that I'd conjured in my imagination.

Time passes in the blink of an eye as I continue to spill my thoughts onto the page, and by the time I finally look up, I'm surprised to find that I've filled almost a third of the notebook. I'm elated - my writer's block is gone! I've never written so much so fast in my life.

The clock on the wall chimes 1 am, and I figure James has probably decided to either stay out with Paul or return to his flat for the night, so I leave my notebook on the coffee table and go to bed.

I WAKE up bright and early, but I don't feel tired. My brain has been working overtime, coming up with scenarios and ideas for the story I'm writing. It's not a historical romance like I usually write. In fact, I guess you could call it a standard contemporary romance. My publisher might not be happy, but at least I've broken the block and started to write again.

I grab my dressing gown and walk into the kitchen to make a quick breakfast of toast and orange juice before returning to the sofa and opening my notebook. I quickly scan the last chapter I'd written the night before and start writing again. The words flow out of me with so much ease. I don't know if what I'm writing is any good or even if I'll show it to anyone, but it feels incredible to finally be able to do the one thing I love the most again.

As lunchtime approaches, I'm startled by a text message from Beth. *James says you've started writing again? This is fantastic news! Pop down to the coffee shop later if you're free. I want to hear all about it and have some news of my own to share with you too!*

I can't help but smile. A coffee and a quick break away from my book would probably do me a world of good, so I quickly type a message back. *See you in an hour :)*

I stand up from the sofa and stretch my limbs, proud of how much I've managed to write in about 24 hours. I must have written about 20,000 words over the last day, and I have some great ideas for moving my story forward. It's just the end that I'm struggling with. I want it to have a happy ending, but I'm not sure if my story will.

I grab the plate and glass I'd used for my breakfast, ready to take them through to the kitchen, when I notice a stiff, white envelope lying on the welcome mat. I pick it up, turning it over in my hands, and my stomach drops. My name is written in bold black lettering. It's not James' writing. He's been here again.

I hurriedly drop the breakfast dishes on the counter and let myself sink to the floor. *You can do this, Ella,* I tell myself. *You don't have to be afraid anymore.*

I rip open the envelope quickly, not wanting to let fear control me and read.

Involving the police was a mistake. You will pay for this.

So, he knows, does he? How is that even possible?

I race down the hallway, my fingers clumsily unbuttoning my shirt as I make it to my bedroom. I fling open my dresser drawers, frantically throw some clothes on, and jam my feet into a pair of trainers. Keys jangle in my shaking hands as I grab my purse and dash out the door. I jump into the driver's seat and slam the door shut, backing out of the driveway and heading straight to the police station. I know Beth will be waiting, but this is something I have to do.

I pull up to the car park at the police station, the letter still tightly gripped in my hand, and get out. Fear is weighing heavy on my chest as I walk into the building, but I'm determined not to let it get the better of me again. Not now. I can do this.

Inside, the station is busy, and I'm greeted by the deputy I spoke to yesterday, Alex Pritchard.

"Good afternoon, Ella," she says as she sees me. "How are you doing today?"

"Not great," I reply, placing the envelope on the reception desk.

"Can I please speak to somebody that's working on my case? I've had another letter."

Her expression softens as she looks down at the letter. "Yes, of course. Just follow me to one of the waiting rooms, and I'll be right with you. Coffee?"

"No, thanks," I reply, just wanting to pass this new information over as soon as possible and leave.

"Ok, I won't be two ticks."

I watch as she leaves the room, and I try to slow my breathing. I turn the envelope over in my hands, trying to figure out how my stalker could have any idea that I've spoken to the police.

Before long, PC Pritchard returns and takes a seat opposite me. She's brought a tape recorder and busies herself setting it up. "This is so that you can talk freely, Ella; you're ok with me using it, right?"

"Yes," I say, not caring one way or another.

"Ok, good. I'll type everything up after we're done talking." She stops for a second to turn the tape recorder on and sits down. "So, you've received a new letter?"

"Yes, this morning."

I watch as she puts on a pair of gloves and takes the letter in her hands, reading the short threat contained within.

"Do you have any idea what time?"

"It could have been any time between 8.30 am and 11 am. I was in the other room and didn't hear it drop."

"Ok, and you didn't hear a car or any other vehicle near your property?"

"No," I say, which means he must have travelled to me on foot. He can't be living that far away. "Have you made any announcements about this case?"

"Announcements? What do you mean?"

"Like, to the media or I don't know. I feel a bit silly asking, but he's found out I've spoken to you, and I've hardly told anyone."

"Not that I'm aware," she replies, pondering my question. "Who have you told?"

"My boyfriend, his two closest friends, and my best friend."

"Ok, can you give me their full names, please?"

"Surely they haven't got anything to do with it?" I say, my mind aghast.

"It would be best for us to check all avenues," PC Pritchard replies. "We can rule them out pretty quickly if they have alibis."

I'm stunned as I pass over their names, refusing to believe that any of them could be my stalker. James, Paul and Beth didn't even know about this until recently, and Jess had been the main person helping me deal with it when I lived in York.

Once I've passed over the information PC Pritchard asks for, I stand to leave, the worn leather of the seat creaking beneath me. As I step towards the door, PC Pritchard reminds me to phone 999 if I notice anyone suspicious on my property and lets me know she'll contact me as soon as she has any further information. I nod my head in acknowledgement, my mind still churning with the possibility that someone I know could be involved. There's absolutely no way.

There's a chill in the air as I leave the station, and I hug my coat around me tightly before making the short drive to Beth's coffee shop.

When I step inside, I'm greeted by a wall of noise and warm air and have to take a second to let my eyes adjust to the light. The place is busy, and the smell of roasted coffee beans fills the air.

"Hello!" I yell as I move through the patrons and towards the coffee counter where Beth is standing.

"Hey, Ella, you made it! I was starting to think you wouldn't be able to tear yourself away from your writing for a minute."

I laugh and take my coat off, the warmth of the coffee shop making me feel so much better than I had twenty minutes earlier.

"Had to make a pitstop on the way here," I say. "Sorry I'm a bit late."

"Not a problem. What can I get you?"

"Just a coffee would be good," I say. "Black, lots of sugar." My eyes are beginning to feel sleepy after my late night, and I could do with a little pick-me-up.

"Coming up," Beth replies, and I watch as she busies herself behind the counter. She passes me my coffee and refuses to take my money.

"You're my favourite author. I'm not charging you while you're in writing mode," she laughs. "Go on, grab us that table in the corner, and I'll get Kirsty to take over for an hour so we can catch up."

I smile, carry my warm drink to the table she'd indicated, and sit down, resting my coat on the chair behind me.

"Fucking awful news about James, isn't it," Beth says as she joins me at the table. "I can't get my head around it."

"Same," I reply. I'd been struggling with knowing what to say to him over the past couple of days, not wanting to say the wrong thing. "He's asked me to treat him like normal, but I don't know if I'm doing that well or not."

"He said the same to Paul and me," Beth replies, her face forlorn. "Paul is in bits. They've known each other since they were kids, and hardly a day goes by where they don't speak to each other. Still, I'm glad he has you. He seems really smitten."

I can't help it, but I blush. "I like him too," I reply honestly. "He said he wishes we'd met years ago, and I can't help but think the same. Still, I'm not losing hope in him yet. He's agreed to go through with the chemo and anything else he's offered to fight this, and the doctor he saw sounded hopeful."

"Fucking chemo," Beth says, placing her mug down on the table harder than expected. "My granddad went through it a few years back, and the side effects are awful. I can't bear to see him going through all that."

"I'll help with as much as I can," I promise.

"I know you will love. We all will. It's just so hard, isn't it?"

Beth looks like she's going to cry, and I reach out and hold her hand over the table, showing my support.

"Anyway," she wipes a tear from her eye. "Where did you have to go that was more important than coming straight to your Whitby bestie?"

"Ah," I reply, half thankful for a change of topic. "I had another letter posted through the door this morning. I took it to the police station."

"You didn't?" Beth replies, her eyes wide and her mouth agape. "What did it say this time?"

"It was short. Mentioned that he knew I'd gone to the police and that I'd regret it."

"Shit, babe. I wonder who the hell could be doing all of this?"

"The policewoman I spoke to seems to think it's someone I know," I replied. "I don't think that, for what it's worth, but she said they haven't made any announcements, so he's found out somehow."

"Who have you told?" Beth asks.

"Only you, James and my best friend, Jess. I trust all of you, and you and James didn't even know me when all of this started."

"And Jess?"

"She doesn't even live around here," I say. "There's absolutely no way she'd drive all the way from York just to drop a letter through my door and drive back. Plus, she's been encouraging me to go to the police since this all started."

"It's all bizarre," Beth agrees. "I wonder if it's someone who's part of the police force. You hear about it from time to time, don't you?"

"Yeah, could be, I guess," I say. "But they'd have had to have been here all along. It doesn't make any sense."

"Well, I hope they manage to figure it out. How long does computer forensics usually take?"

"No idea. And if he's using a VPN, I have no clue how they will manage to trace him."

I shake my head, and Beth squeezes my hand for support. "You've got so many people on your side, Ella. They'll figure it out, I'm sure."

"I hope so," I sigh. "So, what was this news you had to share with me?"

I take a sip of my coffee, enjoying the sensation as it slides down my throat, leaving a comforting warmth in its wake.

"Can you keep a secret?" Beth asks, a twinkle in her eye.

"Of course!"

"Ok, well, I've been planning my wedding to Paul for forever. We got engaged like six years ago, but weddings are so expensive, you know, and I keep changing my mind about what I want. Anyway, I spoke to Paul, and with James being the way he is right now, we've decided to stop putting it off and just do the deed."

"That's amazing news," I say. "Congratulations!"

"Thanks," Beth blushes. "I haven't got all the details planned out yet, but Paul is going to ask James to be his best man. I was wondering if you'd have the time to help me plan everything? We'll probably try and do it in the next couple of months, so there's a lot to do!"

"Oh wow. Yes, I'd love to help you," I say. "Have you got any ideas for a location yet?"

"I think an outside wedding would be nice, especially now the weather is getting warmer. We just need to find the perfect spot. And then I could hold the reception here in the cafe. We won't be inviting many people to keep the costs down."

"What about the cliff near my house?" I say, my mind thinking of all the possibilities. "You'd be more than welcome to change into your dress at mine, and I can make room for a bridal party and anything else you need."

"Oooh, this sounds fantastic!" Beth replies. "I knew getting you involved with this would be a good idea."

I laugh. "Happy to help."

22

JAMES

I gingerly spoon a bite of penne onto my fork, savouring one of my last few meals without the cloying taste of chemotherapy drugs taking over my senses. The ache in my side has been growing in intensity throughout the day, but I'm doing my best to ignore it and focus on committing to memory the flavour of the fresh marinara sauce Ella spent much of the afternoon creating.

"It's delicious," I tell her, forcing a smile onto my lips.

The thought of starting chemotherapy on Monday looms in my mind, and I pause to savour the two days I have left with my girl before my life is flooded with the treatment's terrible side effects.

It's weird. I'm dealing with a terrible illness, but the forced time off work has given me so much time to focus on the things that really matter in life. I've also been able to spend a lot more time with Ella than I would have been able to had I not been ill. Small blessings, I guess.

"I'm glad you like it," Ella replies before breaking off a piece of garlic bread and gracefully chewing it. God, she's so gorgeous.

I met with a police sergeant earlier today regarding Ella's stalker. She'd warned me that it might happen, but I was still surprised by how thoroughly they investigated me. I'd been able to show them the

GPS on my phone, though, showing that I was at Paul's house when the letter was dropped off, and they seemed to think that was enough of an alibi to drop it. Whoever was doing this to her was going to regret it.

"Is Jess still coming over tomorrow?" I ask Ella. A million thoughts run through my head regarding her best friend, and I've been doing my best to keep my suspicion to myself, but it's getting more and more difficult.

"Yeah, I think so," she replies. Her eyes remain focused on the plate in front of her, and I can't help but think she's hiding something from me. "I've not heard from her, and I'm sure she'd say if she had a change of plans. She knows I need my phone back."

"Guess that means you don't know what time she'll be here then?" I say, probing gently.

"No. I'll send her a text in the morning and find out. Don't feel like you can't stay, though! She won't be staying for long if she does come."

I smile at her and spoon another bite of penne onto my fork, the pain in my side feeling more intense with every second that passes.

"James? Are you ok?"

Before I can answer, Ella gets up and walks around the table to me. She takes my hand in hers, and I wince as I try to push the pain away.

"Sorry," I mutter. I drop my fork and feel sweat beading on my brow.

"Do you want to go and lie down?" she asks. "We can watch a movie, or you can watch the football highlights while I write if you'd like?"

"Yeah, that sounds good," I say. I force a strained smile and, with great effort, push myself off the chair. My feet feel heavy as I follow Ella to the living room sofas. I lay down with a thud, and before I can blink, she's vanished, returning a few seconds later with a glass of water in one hand and the TV remote in the other.

"How much do you know about Jess's childhood?" I ask her, my tongue suddenly growing a mind of its own. I chastise myself the instant I let the question slip.

"Not a lot. Why?" Ella asks, looking at me suspiciously. She takes a seat next to me on the sofa and picks my legs up, resting them on her knees.

"It's just, the more I think about things, the more I can't help but think she's involved in this somehow."

"I've known her for ten years, James. She's never given me any indication that I can't trust her. I've gone through everything over and over in my mind, too, and there's so much that doesn't make sense, but I still don't think she'd do this to me."

"Yeah, I'm sure you're right," I reply.

"What was she like when you knew her?" Ella asks me. She gazes into my eyes, and I can see she wants honesty. "You said you had different friendship groups, didn't you? Was there more to it than that?"

"Yes and no," I reply. I take a sip of my water now that the pain in my side has begun to subside. "We did have different friendship groups, and I didn't know her personally. I mean, we went to school together, but I didn't know her to talk to aside from saying the odd hello."

"Go on," Ella urges.

"She left before we finished the last year. Her closest friends said she'd moved to York. Really inopportune timing, but these things happen. But then a rumour started that she was seeing an older man who had got her pregnant and that's why she left in such a hurry. She lived in a foster home, you know, so it's not like her carers would have just up and moved. I guess it gave the whole theory some weight, you know?"

"Jesus," Ella replies, trying to digest everything I've told her. "Well, I can tell you that she hasn't had a child for as long as I've known her."

"It could just be a rumour," I reply. "It really was a shock seeing her again after all these years."

"I can imagine," Ella mutters, and I can tell she's trying to think things through in her head.

"I still don't understand how any of this would mean that she'd be the one stalking me, though," Ella says, as much to herself as to me.

"I'm not sure either," I reply honestly. "But you've gotta admit; it's all a little weird. Just like this situation you're in now."

I SPEND a lovely Sunday morning with Ella, relaxing on the sofa while she writes her novel by my side. It's fantastic to see her doing the thing she loves again, and I love watching her work. The way she rests her head on one hand as she scrawls away, occasionally pausing to look out of the window in deep thought, is mesmerising to me. I make her the odd cup of tea while she writes, enabling her to continue without worrying about anything. I love being able to do this with her.

As lunchtime draws close, I say my goodbyes to Ella and walk outside to my car. I'll be back tonight once Jess has left. I don't want to make awkward small talk with her right now. Plus, Paul and Beth have invited me for Sunday dinner, and I can never say no to a home-cooked roast.

A group of seagulls caw quietly above my head as I drive away from Ella's house, and I can't help but stop the car and look up at them for a moment. Their dirty white plumage is beautiful and almost majestic. I sometimes wish I could fly like them. I'd leave my old life behind and take Ella with me.

I start the car again and meander down the dirt drive towards the main road that will take me to Paul and Beth's house, lost in my thoughts.

As I pull up outside their cottage, I notice Paul in the front garden waiting for me. He looks like he has something on his mind.

"Hey mate, what's up?" I say as I get out of the car.

"Just wanted to talk to you quickly before you go inside and see

Beth," Paul says, his hand now on my shoulder, steering me away from the cobbled path that leads to their front door.

"O..k.." I say, slowly wondering what the hell this could be about.

"Look, mate, we've had the police round here all morning, questioning our whereabouts. They seem to think we could be involved with Ella's stalker. Beth's pretty shaken up about it."

"Yeah, I had to speak to them yesterday," I say. "I don't think there's anything to worry about, though. We're obviously not involved."

"I know, mate, but we've all got the same alibi that we were all together."

"Yeah, and our phones show exactly where we were. Don't worry. Absolutely nothing about this being down to us adds up. They probably just want to strike us from their suspect list."

"Yeah, I suppose you're right," Paul answers calmly. "Beth's pretty shaken up about it, however. She's not used to being interrogated. Just go easy on her today, yeah?"

"When am I not?" I laugh, slightly affronted. "There is one person, though, who I think might be a part of this. I'll tell you and Beth together; I'd like your opinion on whether I'm crazy or not."

Paul leads me inside through the red front door, and the smell of cooking instantly fills my nostrils. I will never not love the smell of roast beef.

"Hello, lovely!" Beth calls from the other room. "Dinner won't be long; I just got a bit held up with it. I'm doing the gravy now and will be right out."

"No worries," I shout back. "It smells delicious!"

"So, how are you feeling now, mate?" Paul asks as I join him in the dining room. "Tomorrow's quite a big day, huh?"

"Yeah," I sigh. "Not really looking forward to it, but what can you do?"

"Hey, it'll be ok," Paul says, slapping me on the back. "You'll get through this; I'm sure of it."

He pulls out a chair for me, and I sit down while Beth enters with a steaming hot plate of food. We spend the next hour or so talking about anything and everything while eating delicious food as if nothing else in the world matters. It's a refreshing break from all the worry and stress I've been carrying around with me lately.

"So, James reckons he might know who's behind the whole stalker thing," Paul says, and I watch Beth's eyes increase in size.

"Ooh, do tell," she encourages me. "Paul's probably already told you that we had the police round here earlier interrogating us. I was half expecting them to take us down to the station. It right scared me it did."

"Sorry about that," I reply, although I don't know what I have to be sorry about. For introducing Ella to them, I guess? Though it's not her fault either.

"So, who do you think is responsible?"

"Well, Ella received another letter the day I was round here - I'm not sure if the police explained that or not? Anyway, the letter contained a threat saying that she'd regret going to the police. But, as far as either of us knows, the only people aware of her reporting the harassment are the three of us sitting around this table and her best friend, Jess."

"So, you think it's the best friend?" Beth asks, entirely focused on me.

" I think it's somebody that knows her, and it's someone that's able to track her movements. The only thing I'm struggling with is that she apparently lives in York. She has a job and a life there, so travelling over here just to keep scaring Ella makes no sense."

"Is this the girl I saw at the harbour?" Paul interjects.

"Yes. And, weirder still is that we went to school with her. Remember a Jessica Beaver?"

"Jesus," Paul remarks.

"What was she like?" Beth asks, looking between us.

"Um, she was,"

"A bit of a nutter," finishes Paul. "She had a close friend for most of our time at the academy. Susie something. Anyway, something happened, and Susie ended up switching schools. Jess left soon after that, and we never saw her again."

"Do you remember the pregnancy rumour?" I ask Paul.

"Yeah! I don't know how true it was. Everyone exaggerated at that age, didn't they?"

"Ella said she's known her for ten years and doesn't have a child, so it probably wasn't true. But it's weird, though, right? Ella seems sure she's not involved, and the last time I saw her, she encouraged her to go to the police. But nothing else makes sense."

"There's no way it could be this Susie girl, could it?" Beth asks. I can see her trying to work it out too. "I mean, girls don't tend to forget things. Could she have been doing it because she's jealous of Ella?"

"It's possible," I reply. "But it's been 15 years since all this went down. I'd hope she's living her life and not still worried about a secondary school falling out."

"I don't like to gossip about people," Paul begins. "But Jess wasn't exactly the sharpest tool in the box, was she? Maybe as time's gone on, she's grown bitter and is doing this to get her revenge."

"If that's true, then why involve Ella? And revenge for what?" I ask.

"Jealousy," he states again, seemingly refusing to let the idea go. "Maybe she was jealous of Susie and did something to her back when we were at school and is now doing the same again."

"I think you're both being a little bit far-fetched, if I'm honest," Beth says as she stands up and cleans the table. "Jess would have to be a real psycho to do stuff like this to someone she's been best friends with for ten years. Girls don't act like that."

23

ELLA

James has only been gone ten minutes when I hear the throaty sound of an engine drawing close. I peek out the window and see Jess's black Jeep carefully rolling up the narrow dirt track that leads to my cottage. Its big tires kick up dust, and I can't help but think the ruggedness of the vehicle seems to belong in this rural setting as if it's a wild animal, finally coming home after a long absence.

I quickly move away from the window and open the door as she parks in the spot recently abandoned by James. I'm excited to see my best friend again after such a long break.

As soon as she climbs out of her car, I'm at her side, welcoming her with an enormous hug. "I'm so glad you could make it! I have so much to catch you up on."

"Can't wait," Jess replies. She sounds enthusiastic, but I can't help but notice how tired she looks. She has large bags under her eyes, and her typically bouncy curls are limp and lifeless. I wonder what's been keeping her up at night. "Cup of tea would be nice first, though," she says as she takes my arm.

I rest my hand on her arm and lead her through the front door of my cottage. It surely looks the same as it did the last time she was here, except for maybe a few more of James' belongings dotted about the place. One thing has changed, though, and that's me. Since the police took my case and I've not had to read the emails and text messages my stalker has been sending, I've been feeling a whole lot better.

I walk through to the kitchen and put a pot on the stove to boil. Jess follows me and slumps into one of the breakfast chairs lining the counter.

"Long weekend?" I ask her.

"Ugh, I couldn't explain it to you if I tried. I'm struggling to keep my eyes open. Honestly was a bit worried I'd end up falling asleep at the wheel on the way over here."

"I'm sorry, Jess," I say as I sort out some tea bags. "You shouldn't have put yourself in danger. You could have posted my phone. It's a long way to come for one afternoon."

"It's ok. Here." Jess slides my phone across the counter to me, and I pocket it, making sure it's turned off first.

"Thanks. Is everything ok with you? Your boss wasn't mad that you had to leave early today, was she? I mean, it is a Sunday and-"

"No, she was fine. Honestly, stop asking about my job Ella. They're very understanding of my need to keep leaving with zero notice."

I pour the hot tea into our mugs and pass one to Jess. "Do you want to tell me what's going on then? Because I can tell something is. You're acting strange, and if it's not to do with work, then it's got to be something else important."

Jess hesitates for a moment before speaking. "Sorry. It's just been a long few weeks. It's been really busy at work, I've been looking for a new place to live, and I've been missing my bestie. I really need some time off and a good night's sleep. That's all it is, I promise."

I'm not convinced, but I know that prying further isn't going to help me find out what's bothering her. If she wanted me to know, she would tell me. I am tempted to email her boss, though and apologise for the constant interruptions. If her boss understands what Jess has done for me over the past few months, it might help.

I pick up my mug of tea and take it into the living room, encouraging Jess to follow me.

"Hang in there," I tell her once we're sitting down. "It won't be like this forever."

"Fingers crossed that's true," she laughs. "What about you then? Have the police got any leads yet on your stalker?"

"No," I frown. "They haven't given me much information except to tell me they're still working on it. My laptop is having some forensics done on it to see if they can work out where the emails have come from."

"Be difficult to tell if he's using a VPN," Jess says flippantly.

"Yep, I'm not holding out much hope. He did take a photo of James and me last weekend and email that to me, so I'm hoping the CCTV might have caught him. Or at least I hope it's given the police a few potential suspects to question."

"Sounds like he's stopped being careful," Jess replies. She takes a mug of her tea, and there's an awkward silence while she drinks. "Hopefully he'll slip up again soon and give them more to go on. So, you and James, huh? It's getting serious?"

"Well, that's the other thing I wanted to talk to you about in person-"

"Oh god, he hasn't told you about what I was like at school, has he?" she laughs, but the smile doesn't reach her eyes. "Don't believe a word of it, Ella. It's not true."

I chuckle. "No, it's not that. Although I'm sure you were a real pain in the ass back then. City girl living in a seaside town. It can't have been easy for you."

"Uh-uh. Why do you think I escaped as soon as I got the chance?"

"You never did tell me about that," I say, hoping to get some information from her that will put James' mind at rest. "What happened?"

"Oh, you know. School wasn't really for me, so I used to go down to Scarborough every chance I got to party. I met a guy there, and when he offered me a way out, I jumped."

"Really?" I say while trying to pretend I haven't heard this story before. "You just left school?"

"Uh-huh. It sounds a bit dumb now that I'm saying it out loud, but I thought it was a great decision at the time."

"How did he afford to support you? Was he a lot older than you?"

"Not that much older," she replies thoughtfully. "He was in his twenties, and I was nearly 17. Was one of those things that seemed like a good idea but ended up not being."

"God, I can't even imagine," I say. 29-year-old me finds the thought both brave and incredibly stupid.

"Yeah, he got arrested not long after we'd moved to York. I considered coming back to Whitby, but my foster parents had had about enough of me by then, so I found a job and lived in a hostel for a while. Plus, his family were from Whitby too, and I didn't want to have to deal with them if I saw them."

"Jesus, Jess. That sounds so scary. I had no idea how much you went through."

"Made me the person I am today, didn't it?" she smiles. "Honestly, if I had the chance to do it all again, I'd probably think twice about it, but also, knowing me, I'd probably go and make the same mistakes. It's just who I am."

I feel a chill run down my spine, and I'm not quite sure why. Jess has been honest with me, but I feel like there's more she's not telling me. Still, I can't mention the pregnancy without her thinking I've been gossiping about her, and I don't want that. She's opened up to me today, and that's all I could have asked for.

"So," Jess probes. "Are you going to tell me more about what's been going on with James?". She picks up his black beanie and throws it at me. "Is he living here now, or are you just into wearing his clothes?"

"Ha ha, very funny." I throw the hat back at her.

"So?"

Fuck, I have no idea how to actually say this. I guess just be honest. "He's been diagnosed with cancer."

"No!" Jess says, the shock evident on her face.

"Yeah. He's starting chemotherapy tomorrow. He's been staying with me a lot since he got the news."

"How is he coping with it?" she asks, and her voice seems full of genuine concern.

"About as well as he can," I reply. "He's putting a brave face on it mostly. It's hard to get a read on him most of the time."

"Shit, Ella, I'm sorry. Why didn't you tell me?"

"It's the kind of news that's best to hear in person, isn't it? I mean, I would have told you if you hadn't come up this weekend, but I'm glad I could tell you face to face."

"I didn't know James well," Jess starts. "But he always seemed like an alright guy when we were at school. It's fucking shit that he has to deal with this so young. Didn't his dad die of cancer too?"

"Yeah, when he was a baby," I reply. "It's just shit all around."

We spend the rest of Jess's short visit catching up about banal things, just to have something light to talk about. Jess tells me about a new guy that she's been dating, and he seems really into her, which is great. I mention my growing stash of fruit and veg thanks to Steve at the market and let her know I've started writing again, which she seems shocked about.

When it's time to say goodbye, I give her a big hug and thank her again for travelling such a long way to see me just to give me my phone back.

"Take care of yourself," she says as she walks to her car. "And let me know if the police have any updates on your case."

"I promise I'll let you know," I reply.

The sun sinks low in the sky as I wave her off and watch as her Jeep trundles away until it's out of sight. I turn back to my house and realise that in a short time, she has made me feel so much better, even if we've only had time for a brief catch-up. I guess some friendships are like that; no matter how long you spend apart, you can pick up right where you left off. She has absolutely nothing to do with my stalker, I'm sure of it.

With a heavy heart, I head back into my house and prepare for another night of worrying about James and what the future holds for us.

24

JAMES

My body feels like a ton of bricks as I collapse onto Ella's sofa, my third chemotherapy session now behind me. I try to sit up, but my body begs for rest. The nausea is overwhelming, but I know I'm going to have to wait until it passes.

"I'm so sorry," I say to Ella, hoping she knows how much it's killing me inside for her to see me like this.

"Shh, you have absolutely nothing to apologise for."

Ella's hands rub soothing circles on my back while she calmly offers words of encouragement. For the first time since my diagnosis, I allow myself to be vulnerable and accept the comfort that she has to offer.

"I don't know if I can keep doing this," I murmur, my voice cracking.

"You don't have to. We can stay here until the sickness passes. It's okay," she whispers into my ear.

I take a deep breath and wince as pain shoots through my stomach. "No, I mean this whole thing. The chemotherapy, everything..." I trail off, shaking my head in defeat.

"James, you're a fighter," she responds, pulling me in closer to her body as she lays on the sofa beside me.

"Not anymore," I respond with a sigh. "I knew the chemo wouldn't be easy, but it's starting to feel unbearable. I don't care about the physical stuff, like losing my hair, but the nausea is on another level. Two shit weeks followed by one semi-good one? I can't deal with another nine weeks of this."

Ella's eyes well with tears as I speak, and I hate that I'm causing her so much pain.

"James, please," she says, and I can feel my heart breaking. "I am so sorry you have to deal with this; I really, really am. If I could take your pain away, I would do so without thinking twice. You're halfway through it, though. Please don't give up now."

It's been getting harder and harder to keep my promise to them all, especially in the days following the treatment. "I want to keep my promise," I say. "It's just getting hard."

Ella doesn't say a word. Instead, she lets out a deep, muffled cry as she burrows her head into my chest. I can feel her body shaking, her breath coming in ragged gasps.

I wrap my arms around her, wanting to take away her pain, but I mean every word I say. This treatment is the most brutal thing I've ever experienced in my life, and how so many people manage to push themselves through multiple courses of it, I don't know.

Her words come out choked, "I just can't lose you."

I kiss the top of her head and try to ease her heartache. "Don't worry, sweetheart. I'm not going anywhere just yet."

She pulls away from me to look into my eyes as if analysing my reactions. Her eyes are so full of uncertainty that I take a sharp intake of breath when she speaks again.

"No... James, you don't understand," She touches my face to make sure I'm listening closely. "I can't lose you. I can't live without you. The last few weeks have been some of the hardest but also happiest in my life. I've fallen in love with you." Her voice is trembling as she speaks, and her eyes are red with tears.

"I love you too, Ella. More than you'll ever know." I pull her in for a kiss, our lips meeting in a moment of raw passion. Despite the crippling side effects currently taking hold of my body, the room fades away as we pour all our emotions into this kiss.

"I know we haven't been together long, but... I can't imagine my life without you," she says, her voice soft and vulnerable.

The tears in her eyes make my heart ache even more. "I feel the same way," I reply, reaching up to wipe away a tear that's cascading down her face.

"Please don't give up," she whispers against my lips.

But I can't find it in me to promise her the one thing she's asking, so I just hold her close, the comfort as much for me as it is for her.

MY ARMS SHAKE with effort as I hurry around Ella's tiny cottage, picking up discarded items and dusting surfaces. I still feel weak and nauseated from the chemo and the chat with Ella last night, but the prospect of seeing Beth and Paul has cheered me up. Ella has invited them over for lunch, and I can't help but feel happy at how well they've been getting along lately.

Although she's offered numerous times, I've insisted that Ella not accompany me to my medical appointments, partly out of pride but also to spare her from the depressing atmosphere surrounding them. To keep her occupied, I suggested she visit Beth's coffee shop and focus on her writing. They'd grown close since then, and I was sure the friendship benefitted Beth just as much as it did Ella.

We've just about finished cleaning when I hear a knock at the door. I muster as much strength as I can to join Ella in greeting our friends and inviting them inside.

"You didn't have to clean for us, mate," Paul says as he steps inside and pats me on the back in welcome. I smile and move to the side to let Beth give me a hug.

"How are you feeling?" she asks me. "You don't look too great."

"Oh, you know," I reply, a stilted smile on my face.

"Why don't you and Paul go and sit down, and I'll get some

drinks," Ella tells me. "It's lovely and warm outside today if you want some fresh air?"

"Fancy it?" I say to Paul.

"Sure, sounds good."

I lead him outside to the small picnic table Ella's landlord and his son had brought over last weekend. They'd placed it to the left of the property, giving us a gorgeous view over the rocky coast below.

"So, how are you really, mate?" Paul asks me as we sit down.

"Honestly? I don't think I can carry on like this," I say to him, hoping he'll receive my news better than Ella did but also wanting to be fully honest. He's been my best friend for as long as I can remember, and he deserves to know the truth.

Paul stares out to sea, his gaze distant and thoughtful as he considers my words. I allow my gaze to follow his and look out over the distant horizon, watching the waves coming alive in a gentle dance against the rocks. The sun breaks through the thin clouds and warms my skin, filling me with contentment.

"I'm going to say this only once, mate, and it's up to you how you take it," Paul finally answers me. "You've got a girl in there that's worth fighting for. She worships the ground you walk on and would do literally anything you ask of her. You have nine weeks left. No one is going to sit here and tell you it won't be fucking hard, ok? We all know it is. We can all see it. But if you can last just nine more weeks, you have a chance of entering into remission and spending your whole life with that lady through there who makes you so happy."

I frown, slightly disappointed that he didn't back my decision. "Guess I've got to force myself to be more optimistic then, huh?"

"Mate, we are all here for you, and we will fight for you every second of every fucking day. Just get through this round, please! If not for you, for the rest of us who can't bear to lose you. Ok?"

"Ok," I nod, hoping that I can do as he asks.

"I assume you've told Ella what you've been thinking?"

"Told me what?" Ella says as she joins us outside with Beth and four ice-cold glasses of lemonade—the perfect drink for a warm spring day.

I sigh, not wanting to upset her again while our friends are here.

"What?" she repeats as she sits beside me and takes my hand.

I suddenly feel a wave of nausea hit me and hold my hand up to stall Ella's questions. I take a sip of the lemonade she's brought me and try to compose myself, but the crispness of the lemons makes my mouth pucker and my stomach turn.

"James, are you ok?" Beth asks as she joins us at the table. "You don't look so good."

"It's the damn chemo," I reply angrily. "I'm sick of it making me feel like this. It's not worth it."

I swallow down the bile rising in my throat. I shouldn't be surprised that I feel like this, the nurse from the oncology department had told me that this was a common side effect, but I had no idea it would be so relentless.

I watch as Ella hurries back to the cottage, her footsteps padding softly against the sand. She returns a minute later and kneels beside me with a cool, damp cloth. She dabs at my forehead and the back of my neck with a gentle touch, and relief fills me as it helps a little.

The silence stretching out between us makes me embarrassed, and I hate that my closest friends have to deal with me like this. I'm thankful when Beth breaks it.

"So, James, me and Paul have some news for you?"

"Oh yeah?" I reply, willing myself to look better than I feel as I focus on what they're about to tell me.

"So, you know how we've been planning our wedding for forever?"

"Literally forever," Paul laughs.

"Well, we've finally booked it."

"And I'd like to ask if you'd stand by me and be my best man?" Paul says, his voice catching slightly as he awaits my response.

"What? When?" I say, shocked that Paul has finally got Beth to make a decision about it.

"The weekend after next," Beth continues, the excitement clear on her face. "We've hired an officiant to perform it here, overlooking the sea. And then I thought we could have a small reception at the coffee shop afterwards."

"Wow, I, uh, I don't know what to say. Congratulations!" I have a feeling that they've been forced to stop taking forever to plan their wedding to make sure I'm there. "Are you just moving this forward because I'll be dead by the time Beth finally makes a decision on the perfect wedding?" I laugh.

"Mate, we'll all be dead by then," Paul chuckles, and Beth hits him in the side. "So, what do you say? Will you be my best man?"

"I'd love to," I reply. "Thank you."

Ella squeezes my hand, and I smile at her, suddenly realising she knew they were going to ask me this today.

"Did you know about this?" I whisper, and she smiles.

"Ella's been helping me sort everything out," Beth replies. "Who knew she was such a good wedding planner?"

I chuckle, grateful they've taken my mind off my illness, even for a moment.

We spend the afternoon enjoying the delicious lunch Ella has prepared for us and talking about Beth and Paul's wedding. No further mention of me stopping chemotherapy is made, and as the sun sets on our little group, I feel a sense of sadness creeping over me. This could be one of the last times we're all together like this if I do give up the treatment.

After saying our goodbyes to Beth and Paul, I let Ella steady me as we walk back from the garden and into her cottage. I smile as she tucks me onto the plump sofa and kisses my damp forehead, leaving me for a moment to reflect on a wonderful evening spent with good friends.

Before I can stop it, my stomach churns again, and I slump back into the pillows, exhaustion and nausea consuming me until every-thing fades away into darkness.

⁓

I CAN JUST ABOUT MAKE out Ella's voice. It's muffled, and there's someone else here, too, shining a light into my eyes.

"He's going to be ok," one of the unknown voices says, and I startle, trying to push them away from me but being too weak to do so.

The familiar scent of Ella's perfume drifts over me, and I ache to hold her close. I open my eyes further and see two paramedics kneeling in front of me. Ella stands just to the side of them, worry overwhelming her features.

"What happened?" I ask.

"You're good now, James," the male paramedic tells me. "Can you stand? We're just going to take you to the hospital and make sure everything's ok."

I try and push myself up from the sofa, trying to make sense of what's happening, but my legs are weak, and I stumble. The paramedics catch me, and everything goes black again. The last thing I remember is lying in the back of the ambulance with Ella quietly sobbing by my side.

25

ELLA

The monotone beeps from the private hospital room pierce the air like a sharp knife as I sit beside James's bed, waiting. I haven't slept a wink since we got here, and my head is spinning from the events of last night. I'd known he'd been struggling, but I hadn't known quite how much.

A nurse comes in to do some observations, and I smile at her, but she doesn't smile back. She's methodical, robotic, like all the hospital personnel on night shift duty. I watch as she presses a cold stethoscope to James' chest before looking up at the monitor. His lean muscles respond more slowly than they should, and I can't help but notice how fragile and thin he looks, his skin almost resembling paper.

My phone vibrates in my pocket as the nurse leaves, and I look down to see Beth is calling. I answer quietly, not wanting the nurse to ask me to step outside.

"Ella? What's going on? I got your message."

"He's ok," I reply softly. "I'm sitting with him now. I think the chemo is just really starting to take its toll on him, and all the socialising yesterday was too much."

"Paul told me James doesn't want to have any more chemo," Beth replies, almost in question.

"Yeah..." I say. "I'm hoping to change his mind."

I stroke James's hand gently and feel a tightness in my chest. I'm not ready to say goodbye to him, but at the same time, I can't watch him continue to suffer like this. "I understand why he feels that way, but maybe there are some other medications that can help with all the side effects he's experiencing."

There's a long silence on the other end of the line, and I can hear Beth taking deep breaths. "Are you going to be okay?" she asks finally.

"I don't know," I say honestly. "I'm scared, Beth. I don't know how to do this without him."

"You don't have to do it alone," she reminds me. "I'm here for you, for both of you."

"Thank you, Beth. That means a lot."

"Let me know when he wakes up, yeah? Or if anything changes."

"I will do. Go and get some sleep."

"Night Ella."

I hang up and pull my writing notebook out of my bag. I turn to the first page, tracing my finger along the lines of text, and smile, remembering the day I started writing again. It had been so easy to forget everything, thanks to my self-imposed tech ban and the support of my new friends. Without thinking any further, I begin to read out loud.

James and Ella: A Seaside Love Story

I fight the tears that threaten to fall as I read the story I've written about me and the man lying in the bed next to me. Unlike our real-life story, this one has hope. It has a future. By the time I've reached the end of the second chapter, tears are brimming in my eyes, and I stop, trying to catch my breath. Suddenly I feel his hand clasp mine.

"Don't stop," he encourages softly. "Keep reading."

I glance at James, and though still pale, the encouragement in his eyes is unmistakable. I'm glad he's awake. Taking comfort in his strength, I tighten my grip on his hand and take a few deep breaths before continuing to read.

James watches me as I recite the words, unmoving except for his hand in mine. I can feel his gaze on me, savouring each word and finding comfort in the fictional love story I've created. As I finish reading the third chapter, he tightens his grip on my hand and whispers, "I love you."

I turn to face him, feeling the tears that have been threatening to spill finally escape. "I love you too," I say, leaning in to kiss him softly.

Despite the heartache and pain of our reality, in this moment, I am grateful for the love we share. It's a love that has endured through sickness and police investigations, and even if it doesn't get to have a happy ending in the traditional sense, it's a love story worth telling.

"I wish I could handle the treatment better," James says, moving his hand to caress my cheek. "I'd do anything to have met you earlier."

"Don't talk like that," I beg him. "You made us all a promise remember? You have to keep fighting this."

"Keep reading," he smiles. "I want to hear what happens."

As I approach the sixth chapter's end, I feel James' grip on my hand loosen. I look up and see that he's fallen asleep again. I close the notebook and tuck it back into my bag, grateful for the brief moments of comfort it provided.

I lift my wrist to check the time, illuminated by the glow of the hospital's lights. The second hand ticks ever closer to 4 am, and I know that sleep is necessary if I'm going to be of any use to James tomorrow. But before I can succumb to exhaustion, I tap my thumb against my phone and start typing a message to Jess.

I wish you lived closer. I really need you right now x

I hit send and slide my phone back into my pocket. I miss being able to talk to Jess as much as I had when we lived in the same city. Beth was becoming an excellent friend, but it was different to the friendship I shared with Jess. Ten years is a long time, and there's so much you get to know about a person over that many years.

I lean back into the hard leather chair of the hospital room and open the blanket that had been draped over it when we arrived, trying to make a comfortable nest for myself in the hopes of catching a few hours of much-needed sleep.

I AWAKE to the sound of a nurse once again doing observations on James. It's a different nurse this time. This one seems a lot friendlier. She has a kind smile.

"Morning, sleepyhead," she says as I rub my eyes, willing them to wake up properly.

The room is lighter now, the sun high in the sky.

"What time is it?" I murmur.

"Just gone 8.30 am. I'm Cathy, and I'll be taking care of James today."

I smile at her. "I'm Ella, his girlfriend. Do you think he'll be able to come home with me today?"

"Ah, I don't think so, love. James isn't doing too well right now, and we're going to look at some pain and symptom management options that will help him. We can only do that here. You're welcome to stay as long as you like, though."

My heart jumps a little at the news.

"Thanks," I reply, trying to smile. "Will you be able to make him more comfortable then? He's been really struggling with the chemo. Says he doesn't know if he can continue."

"Aw, it is brutal love. He's not the first patient to say that either, but most of them do carry on and finish the course. We'll try to gauge better what's hurting him and see if we can change his medication to help."

I thank her and watch as she measures James' temperature and blood pressure. She records the results methodically and places them in a little folder at the end of his bed. Next, she checks that the wires attached to him are secure and that she's not missing anything.

"Right, I'll leave you two alone for a bit," she says to me, a reassuring smile on her face. I like her a lot more than the other nurse. "If he wants anything when he wakes up, just pop down the corridor to the nurse's station. I won't be far away."

I thank her and watch as she bustles out of the room.

Once she's gone, I recheck my phone and am surprised to see a message from Jess. It was sent three hours ago. I can't help but wonder what she was doing awake in the middle of the night. Probably enjoying a night of passion with the new guy she's dating, knowing her. I smile, glad she's found her own slice of happiness and open her text.

What's going on? x

I quickly reply.

James is in the hospital. He's not doing too well. Looks like he's going to be in for a few days x

I hit send and see the three dots on my screen, letting me know she's replying.

Shit, Ella, I'm really sorry. Is there anything I can do? x

I consider asking her to come over, but it's a lot to ask, especially with how busy she is at work at the moment. And I really want James to be able to stay with me when he gets out of here. I don't know how comfortable he would feel being around Jess too. Even after I'd put his mind at ease following her last visit, I still get the impression he doesn't fully trust her.

A call from Beth interrupts my thoughts, and I answer it quickly.

"Hey Ella, any updates?"

"No," I reply. "Not really, anyway. I think they're going to keep him in for a little while to try and get his pain and symptoms under control."

"That sounds like a good thing," Beth reassures me.

"Yeah, I guess so," I say with a sigh. "It's just hard seeing him in so much discomfort."

"I can only imagine," Beth says sympathetically. "Do you need me to come down there and keep you company? I can pop to yours on the way and pick up a spare change of clothes and some snacks if you like?"

I consider her offer for a moment and decide that I would like her here. "That would be amazing. Thank you so much. I really appreciate it."

"Don't mention it. I'll be there in an hour or so. Have you got a spare key lying about or anything?"

"Shit, no, I haven't. My landlord lives close, though; he might be able to let you in. If not, forget about the spare clothes. I'll have to return home at some point today anyway."

"Text me his number, and I'll give him a call."

I glance over at James, his chest rising and falling as he peacefully sleeps.

"I will do, Beth. Thank you so much for this. We're in the oncology ward. Cathy is the nurse taking care of him."

"No problem. See you soon."

I hang up and send Beth my landlord's number before replying to Jess.

No, don't worry. I miss you, that's all x

Seconds later, a new nurse arrives with a plate of toast for James. I gently stroke his hand, encouraging him to wake up.

"There's nothing for family, I'm afraid," she says as she places James' breakfast on the table beside his bed. "There's a café, though, down on the lower level if you're hungry."

"I'm ok," I reply, though I could go for a full English right now.

James slowly opens his eyes and smiles at me as I squeeze his hand.

"Hello, handsome," I say. "How are you feeling?"

"Tired," he replies, his voice raspy. I pour some water into a glass and pass it to him gently. He takes a sip and voices a sigh of relief. "Did they say how long they're going to keep me in here?"

"They're not sure," I reply honestly. "They want to help you feel better, so they're going to look into some symptom management options. Possibly some pain management too."

"Ah, am I getting the good drugs now?" James whispers, a cheeky smile on his face, and I can't help but laugh.

"You are, and they're going to make you feel so much better. I promise."

I reach up and stroke his face; it feels warm and smooth to my touch. He presses his face up against my hand in response, and once again, my chest tightens as I realise just how much he means to me.

"Beth's going to pop over in a bit," I say. "She's offered to bring snacks."

James looks concerned. "I can't believe I've got everyone running around after me."

I sigh, wrapping my arms around myself. "James, you can't think like that. Your friends want to help."

"I guess Beth is the queen of good snacks," he says with a wry smile.

I help him eat some toast and then get him dressed in something other than the hospital gown he's been wearing since he arrived. I should have asked Beth to bring him some clothes in, too; I didn't think. Still, I can nip home and get him some myself in a bit.

I'm just rearranging his pillows to make him comfortable when there's a knock on the door, and Beth enters.

"Heyyyyy," she says, a big smile on her face. "Did someone order snacks and caramel frappuccinos?"

"You didn't!" James says, laughing as he takes his drink from her. "I can't believe you brought these in with you!"

I take my own drink and pull out a chair for her to sit down.

"Thanks, Beth! You have no idea how much I needed this."

Beth places a bag of clothes next to her chair, and we quickly go over everything that's happened. James insists he's feeling a lot better now, but Beth encourages him to remain where he is for a few days.

"If it's going to make you feel better, James, it's worth it. There is absolutely no way I'm letting you give up on us, and I'm sure me and Ella can hang out by your bedside until you're released."

"Yep, there's no way I'll be leaving you," I say, squeezing his hand.

James looks at me with a twinkle in his eyes. "Oh, I don't know how lucky I am to have you two taking care of me," he says, sounding a little flirtatious.

I feel myself blushing but play along. "Well, we aim to please, Mr Handsome Patient," I smirk.

Beth giggles and adds, "Just wait until you see your nurse. You won't know what hit you."

James grins, clearly enjoying the attention. "I can't wait," he says before sipping his frappuccino.

The hours pass by with Beth and I chatting quietly between ourselves while James dozes in and out of sleep. He looks so peaceful when he sleeps, with a slight smile on his face, like he's dreaming about something wonderful. As the day wears on, I find myself becoming more and more restless. Watching him sleep is making me feel even more helpless than I already do.

"Did you manage to get hold of Mr Briars?" I ask Beth once James has nodded off again.

"I did yeah. He was out of town but sent his son to let me in instead. I've got your stuff here." She pats the carrier bag sitting beside her chair. "Did you know his son is the same guy who spoke to us at the bar that first quiz night you joined us for?"

I try to remember. So much has happened since that night. But then I remember. "The guy who creeped me the hell out? Yeah, I remember him."

"Paul sees him quite a bit these days, from what he's said. He enjoys going out on the tourist charters he runs. He's bloody weird, though, if you ask me."

"In what way?" I ask, my heart suddenly racing.

"He wanted to accompany me into your bedroom," Beth replies. "I told him I'd be ok, but he insisted, said he had to, to make sure I didn't steal anything. He seemed nosey too. Was asking a lot of questions about you and James. He was almost acting like he knew you both well."

"I haven't spoken to or seen him in weeks," I reply. "And James was pretty annoyed with him for making up lies that seemed to be intended to cause problems."

"I guess Paul could have been giving him details," Beth replies. "I'll have a word with him tonight."

"Beth, I'm going to head home for a bit," I say, standing up from my chair. "I should have brought James some clothes in too. Would you mind staying with him for a bit longer?"

"Of course not, go ahead," she replies, taking my place at James' bedside. "Are you ok Ella?"

"Yeah," I respond though not really feeling it. "I just have a funny feeling something isn't right, and I want to check something out."

THE CLOCK on the wall strikes 2 pm just as I walk inside my cottage. I quickly rush around, making sure everything is how I left it. And that's when I see it—a new letter on the kitchen countertop.

I tear it open, knowing exactly who's left it here.

He's either really stupid and thinks I'll blame Beth, or he wants me to know he's behind the months of pain I've endured. I quickly grab some of James' clothes and my phone charger and rush out to my car. I don't plan to return to this house alone again.

26

JAMES

I finally relax as Ella's car makes the slow drive up the dirt track towards her cottage. The gorgeous sea view always invokes a sense of calm in me, and although I won't be getting out on the water again any time soon, the water is always where I've felt most at home.

"That's where I want you to place me if I don't make it," I say to Ella softly. "I want to be cremated and have my ashes scattered in the sea. Promise me?"

A tear slides down Ella's cheek as she turns to look at me. She nods her head and wipes it away. "You are going to make it," she says, a look of defiance in her eyes. "But, if something does happen to you years in the future, I promise I'll make it happen."

I'd spent a total of five days in the hospital, and there were now only a few days left until Paul and Beth's wedding. I'd been a pretty terrible best man by all accounts, but Beth and Ella had spent many an afternoon planning the small details and phoning vendors from the side of my hospital bed. A couple of the nurses had complained at first, but once they realised they weren't going to stop, they left them to it. Nurse Cathy even advised Beth on the best florist to go with at such short notice.

Ella steps out of her car seat and walks around the front of the car to help me out of mine. Thanks to the new medication I've been prescribed, I don't feel as nauseated now, but my legs and body are still weak. With a steady hand, Ella supports my elbow as we slowly make our way up to the cottage and make our way inside, her grip not loosening for even a second. I shuffle over to the couch, barely able to keep my eyes open, while Ella fusses about in the kitchen, making us a pot of tea.

The comforting aroma of Earl Grey soon fills the room as Ella walks in, two steaming cups in her hands. I almost expect her to go and empty the car full of our belongings, but instead, she sits down next to me, and I can tell there's something on her mind.

"What is it?" I ask her as I take a sip of tea, enjoying the lack of nausea as I swallow it easily.

Ella places her mug of tea down on the coffee table and takes my hands in hers. "Ok, this is going to sound really out of the blue, but I know who's been stalking me," she says. Her voice is quiet but firm. She needs to get this out. "I don't know why or understand any of the reasons behind it, but I do know who is responsible."

"Who is it?" I say, my eyes suddenly wide and alert. "Do I know him?"

"His name is Leonard Briars. He's my landlord's son and, apparently, also a friend of Paul's."

"That guy me and Paul took out on the charter that time? No fucking way. How did you find out?"

"When you were in the hospital, I asked Beth to stop by and pick up some clothes for me. She had to ask my landlord to let her in, and Leonard arrived on behalf of his father; she recognised him from the pub but didn't say anything to him. I returned home later that afternoon to pick some bits up for you, and there was a new letter on the counter. Beth didn't put it there, and nobody else can access this house."

"Fuck," is all I can bring myself to say. "I knew there was something dodgy about him but fuck. I'd completely convinced myself that Jess had something to do with it, but if his dad's your landlord. God this makes sense. Have you told the police?"

"Not yet. I didn't want to return here until you were with me, and I wanted to make sure I wasn't going crazy. I've been thinking it over a lot while you slept in the hospital, and while I still have absolutely no idea why he's done all this, I know nobody else could be responsible. And, for what it's worth, I don't think you are entirely wrong about Jess."

I look up at Ella, encouraging her to continue.

"I contacted her boss yesterday to apologise for her needing to take so much time off when I first moved here, and she told me Jess hasn't worked there for six months."

"Jesus. Why would she lie?"

"I don't know, and I haven't asked her yet. I'm hoping she has a reasonable explanation, and she's probably going to be pretty mad that I've spoken to her old boss after she asked me not to. I was trying to help her out, but she won't see it that way, I don't think."

I try to think of a reason why Jess would lie, but my mind comes up blank. I don't know her anywhere near as well as Ella does, and aside from the rumours that circulated about her when we were kids, she hasn't given me any reason not to trust her to have a good explanation. My head is swimming with questions.

I look over at Ella and see the concern on her face before speaking up again.

"What are you going to do next?" I ask her. "Whatever it is, let me help you."

She takes my hand and looks into my eyes. "I think I need to contact the police first," she says. "The Jess situation can wait."

I pass her my phone. There's no time like the present. "Call the station. Ask the officer in charge of your case to come over. Make it clear how urgent it is."

"I should probably just go down there in person," she replies.

"It would be better if they could come here," I urge her. "I want to be there for you through this the same way you have been there for me."

Ella takes the phone from my hand and makes the call.

An hour later and there's a knock on the door. Ella gets up to answer it, and PC Pritchard walks inside with a policeman I don't think I've seen before.

"You have some updates?" she asks as she walks through to the front room. I try to look semi-presentable, but neither police officer mentions how rough I look.

"I, um, I actually think I know who is responsible," Ella says. "Do you want to sit down?"

PC Pritchard sits in the armchair Ella recently vacated while her partner remains standing. Ella joins me on the sofa, and I wrap her hands in mine, giving her the encouragement she needs to continue.

Ella takes a deep breath and then starts speaking. "His name is Leonard Briars. He's the son of my landlord. I don't know exactly where he lives, but I do know he is local to Whitby. I have his father's contact details if that will help."

I squeeze Ella's hand, letting her know she's doing great. The two officers exchange a look before the standing one pulls out a notepad and pen.

"Okay, we'll need you to provide us with a statement detailing everything he's done and why you think he's responsible. We can do that now if you're ok with that? After that, we'll go back to the station and begin an investigation into Mr Briars."

Ella nods and explains everything she knows about Leonard, from the letters to the time she saw him lurking outside her window. My blood boils with anger as she recites everything. I also mention the tourist charter I did with Paul and how he'd been asking me questions I now know were posed to gain more information on Ella.

The police officers listen attentively, taking notes and asking follow-up questions whenever they need more information.

After what feels like an eternity of answering questions and recounting everything that's happened, a heavy knock at the front door interrupts the conversation. I force myself to stand and walk over to answer the door, expecting to see another police officer, but instead, two paramedics are standing there, bag in hand.

The shock is clear on my face.

"I'm guessing you didn't call us," the shorter of the two says.

"Huh?" I reply, confused.

"You called 999 about an hour ago, saying your girlfriend has been assaulted," he continues. "Did she change her mind about needing our help?"

"No! What? No! Ella hasn't been assaulted. We didn't call you because we don't need you."

The paramedic and his colleague exchange another glance.

"Can we come in and see your girlfriend, sir? Just to check everything's ok. If there's no cause for concern, we'll leave."

I open the door and let them enter, showing them through to the front room.

"James, what's going on?" Ella asks.

The paramedics look at the police officers and are given permission to continue. The shorter man speaks again.

"Sorry to intrude, Miss, but we had a 999 call come in saying that your boyfriend was assaulting you. Are you alright? Can you tell us what happened?"

"I'm sorry, but who called you? No one has assaulted me. We only got home from the hospital a couple of hours ago, and I've been with the police ever since then."

"When did you say this call came in?" PC Pritchard asks.

"2.21 pm," the taller paramedic replies.

PC Pritchard looks at her watch. "We were here then. We have no reason to suspect Ella has been assaulted, and neither they nor we called you."

"Could this be him again?" I interject, the pieces falling into place. "Could he know you're here somehow and be trying to frame me, knowing you're close to catching him?"

PC Pritchard nods. "It's a possibility. Can you make a call PC Bowen and find out if you can trace the origins of the call?"

The paramedics apologise for any inconvenience caused and leave through the front door with PC Bowen, but the incident leaves us both feeling shaken.

"I can't believe this is happening," Ella says. "Why won't he just leave me alone?"

"I don't know," I reply, wrapping her in my arms. "But he won't be able to do it for much longer. His time is up."

PC Pritchard finishes tying up Ella's statement and asks her to read through and sign at the bottom. Once done, she stands up and leaves, promising to be in touch as soon as she has further information. I lock the door behind her and return to Ella on the sofa, my arm wrapping its way around her shoulders and pulling her close.

The weight of the day's events is heavy on our shoulders, but I have a surprise for Ella. Or at least, I hope I do if Beth has done what I asked yesterday.

I lean in and press my lips to Ella's forehead, lingering momentarily before walking outside. My eyes land on the large plant pot at the corner of the cottage and a medium-sized package wrapped in brown paper hidden just behind it. "Yes, Beth, you star," I say out loud, and I can't help but feel excited.

I carefully pick the package up and hug it close to my chest. With a deep breath, I open the front door and walk back into the living room and my girl sitting alone on the sofa. She's been through so much since moving here. Not only with her stalker but with me too. She's been there for every step of my journey since my diagnosis, and I want to show her how much she means to me.

"What's this?" Ella asks as I pass the parcel to her.

"Just a little something for my favourite writer," I wink. "Go on, open it!"

I watch as Ella slowly peels the Sellotape from one end of the parcel and eases the box out of the paper.

"You bought me a typewriter?" she asks, a huge grin erupting on her face.

"A smart typewriter," I confirm. "I figured it might be easier on your hands but also eliminates the need to deal with the downside of technology. You can still transfer your manuscripts to your computer when you're done for editing, sending them to your publisher and whatnot."

Ella looks up at me with tears in her eyes. "Oh, James! Thank you so much," she breathes before kissing me softly.

"You promised me you'd finish our story," I remind her as I kiss her back. I feel my body responding to her touch, my desire for her growing stronger with each passing moment. I wrap my arms around her and pull her close, deepening our kiss as my hand slides down her body. "I hope if I continue this round of treatment, it might have a happy ending."

Ella moans into my mouth, pressing herself against me as I move my hand up under her shirt, feeling the smooth skin of her back. I can feel the tension and stress of the day melting away as we kiss, losing ourselves in each other's embrace.

27

ELLA

Beth and I sit joyfully on my living room sofas as the two stylists she'd hired for her big day work their magic on our hair and makeup. Beth had stayed the night in the guest bedroom while James spent the night with Paul at their cottage in town. We'd stayed up late, discussing her excitement for her big day over glasses of champagne and a cosy movie or three. It had been years since I'd enjoyed a proper girls' night.

Yesterday morning, I received an update from the police. They had determined that Leonard Briars was the man responsible for stalking me over the past few months. Not only had the forensics team received a good lead from my laptop, but the information James and I had relayed on Tuesday also allowed them to confirm their suspicions.

Unfortunately, that was where the positive news ended. The bad news was that this wasn't his first charge for a similar crime. He had walked out of prison just 11 months ago, clearly not very rehabilitated. Additionally, they were having difficulty finding him. The only address they had for him seemed to have been recently vacated, and tracking his phone was proving troublesome.

Still, knowing he was a wanted man made me feel better, and I doubted he'd risk coming anywhere near the cottage when the police were after him. My reign of terror was as over as it could be without him actually being locked in a jail cell.

"Up or down. What do you reckon?" Beth asks, distracting me from my thoughts.

"How about a mix of both?" I reply. "An up-do with a few strands curling over your shoulders will look gorgeous."

"What she said," Beth motions to the hair stylist currently increasing the size of her curls for dramatic effect.

We chat excitedly while the stylists continue to work on us, fixing our hair and applying our makeup for the upcoming nuptials, the pampering making me feel like a million dollars. Despite not getting the big ceremony she's always dreamed of, Beth beams with joy.

None of us wanted to risk having a big do with James in attendance. I just hope he has enough strength to make it through the afternoon. He'd been much better since he got home from the hospital, but he was still frail, and most things took it out of him. Still, when I said goodbye to him yesterday, I knew he was determined to make it through his best friend's special day.

"Any word from Jess?" Beth asks me.

"No," I reply. "I've left her a few voicemails and texts, but she's not replying."

I'd given Beth the lowdown on the Jess situation the night before, and she'd helped put things into perspective for me. A ten-year friendship wasn't worth ending over a lie that hadn't affected me personally. I just wished she'd return my calls. I was starting to worry.

"Hopefully she's just holed up with something, and she'll get back to you soon," Beth says sympathetically.

"Yeah, I'm sure that's all it is."

As the stylists finish applying our makeup, I hear cars making their way up towards my cottage. I peer out the window with Beth while she tells me who everybody is.

"That's my parents. That's Paul's dad. Oh, and there's Paul and James. Shit, he can't see me before I'm ready to walk down the aisle."

I laugh and pull the curtain so nobody can see into my cottage.

"Relax, they won't come here."

I sneak another look out the window and watch as Paul helps James out of the car and over to the small altar I'd set up with Beth the night before. A gorgeous array of peonies in shades of pink and white surround the area where they are going to say their vows, and I can't help but think how romantic the whole thing is.

James looks frail but determined as Paul helps him walk over there, his hand gripping his best friend's arm. My heart swells with pride at his bravery, and I'm so glad he's able to experience this day.

A knock on the door breaks me out of my thoughts, and I open it to see Beth's dad standing there.

"All ready, Beth?" he asks her. "I'm so proud of you, darling. You make such a beautiful bride, and Paul is so lucky to have you. He's truly the luckiest guy in the world."

"Thanks, Dad," Beth replies, hugging him. "I can't wait to make it official."

"Come on then. Let's go get you wed."

I take a deep breath and follow them outside into the bright early summer sunshine. Beth's dad takes her arm in his, and together they walk over to the congregation and down the makeshift aisle towards Paul and James. I follow closely behind them with my bouquet of lavender-blue roses tight in my hands as tears spill from my eyes onto the petals.

The sun shines brightly over our heads as we approach Paul, who is waiting eagerly for Beth at the end of the aisle lined up on either side by an archway. He looks so handsome standing there wearing a navy-blue tux with a lilac tie that matches the shade of Beth's dress.

I take a seat on the second row, gently brushing James's shoulders as I sit down to let him know I'm here if he needs me.

Paul cries as Beth lets go of her dad's arm and stands opposite him, ready to make their love official. "You look incredible," he whispers, and she really does. She's foregone the traditional white wedding dress and is instead wearing a gown that seems to have been made just for her. The deep lilac fabric hugs every curve of her body, with tiny floral embroidery adorning the waistline and hem. She's gorgeous.

I dab at the tears flowing freely down my cheeks as Beth and Paul stand in front of their guests, facing each other. The sunlight illuminates their faces, love and joy radiating from them both. They speak their handwritten vows slowly and deliberately, and I feel my heart swell with emotion - an overwhelming mixture of happiness for them and sadness that life hadn't panned out so easily for myself and James.

Finally, the officiant pronounces them man and wife, and they lean in to seal their union with a kiss. Everyone standing up on the cliff top erupts into joyous applause, with cheers filling the room and colourful confetti raining down on the happy couple like a celebration of tiny snowflakes.

As the newlyweds bask in their friends' congratulations, I slowly back away from the laughing crowd and make my way to the cliff edge. The breeze makes me shiver slightly as I look out across the seemingly endless ocean, but my heart feels just as heavy. James stands out among the sea of unfamiliar faces, talking animatedly to Paul and some of his fishing friends. Knowing he's safe and happy allows me a brief moment of solace before I turn away and walk further along the cliff to a more secluded spot slightly hidden by trees.

I sit on a large rock and finally allow myself to cry, letting the mix of emotions I've been holding onto for weeks fall free.

"Hello Ella."

The voice startles me, and I spin around, wiping my tears as quickly as I can.

"What do you want?" I say, trying to make my voice sound more confident than it feels as I look right into the eyes of my stalker. "Had to ruin another happy occasion, did you?"

"You don't look that happy to see me," he smirks. "Didn't your mummy ever tell you not to walk off on your own when a big bad man is on the loose?"

"Leave now, or I will scream," I say, trying to sidestep to get around the rock I'd been sitting on. I couldn't move backwards, not unless I wanted to fall a hundred feet to my death.

My heart rate quickens as he steps closer to me and continues to smirk that awful, soul-destroying grin. I can feel his hot breath on my skin, and I try to force myself not to panic and take another step to the side, increasing the distance between us.

"Why?" I ask him, trying to keep him talking as I regain my composure.

"You know why," he replies, edging another step closer to me. "You didn't deserve any of it. Your book contract, your fans, your friends."

He leans over the rock and grabs hold of my wrist, and I scream, the loudest scream I have ever cried in my life.

"Get off of me!" I shout, kicking my leg out and connecting with the top of his leg. He stumbles back, allowing me to run, but he's too fast. Before I know it, he's wrapped his arms tightly around me, trapping me in his embrace.

"Come on now, Ella," he whispers into my ear. "Let's just have a little fun."

His hot breath makes my skin crawl, and I feel sick with fear. I struggle against him, clawing at his face and trying to escape, but he only tightens his grip.

"Get off me!" I scream again, hoping that someone will hear me and come to my rescue. But the sound is muffled by his hand covering my mouth, trying to keep me silent. I continue to struggle, trying to break free from his hold or kick and bite him when that doesn't work.

The fear that's been gripping my heart since I first heard his voice turns into an all-consuming rage. I'm not some silly little girl who's going to get upset by bad reviews and threatening emails. And definitely not when they're sent by a grown man who still lives with his parents. I don't need his validation, I never have, and he deserves to feel the pain that he's inflicted on me for himself.

My chest heaves as I struggle to breathe, but I manage to muster an ounce of strength which seems to open my eyes wide. In the midst of this fight, I make out Jess's tall frame, standing over by the cars parked near my cottage in the distance.

"Help!" I scream to her, knowing that she is watching us.

Leonard spins me around so she's hidden from my view, but it's too late. The sight of her brings back a memory from the self-defence class we took years ago when we were fresh out of university. The instructor had taught us some moves to get out of this exact situation.

I gather all the strength I have left and swing my elbow back as hard as I can, connecting with his nose and making him lose his grip on me for a second.

I rush back to the cliff as quickly as I can, hoping against all hope that my plan will work. Even if Jess does manage to get help, they won't get here in time.

Leonard rushes towards me, blood pouring from his nose, as the anger he's been feeling towards me all this time takes hold. But I'm not weak anymore. I'm not putting up with his shit any longer.

He barrels towards me; his hands outstretched like claws. I drop to one knee as he reaches me, coiling my body as an anchor. With both hands intertwined around his waist, I use the momentum of his weight and velocity to flip him over my shoulder and into the air. My ears fill with a piercing shriek, followed by a loud thud as his body connects with the rocks below.

I kneel, my ripped dress pooling around me like a shattered halo, and cry. Large deep sobs erupt from my body as I take in the horror of what I've just done. My body is caked in dried blood and dirt, my face covered in scratches. Tears of relief and horror streak down my face as I realise what's happened. What he's driven me to do.

"Ella?"

I look up, and James is standing there, Paul and Beth on one side of him, Jess on the other, a look of pure and utter horror on all their faces.

28

JAMES

My mind stills as I try to make sense of the scene before me. One minute I'm enjoying a cold drink with my best friends, laughing and joking and celebrating their nuptials; the next, Jess is shouting at us that Ella's in trouble.

We run over to her as quickly as we can, no time to even wonder why Jess is here. Despite struggling for breath and my body aching all over, I manage to keep pace with the rest of them as we race over the cliff top to help Ella. But we're too late. None of us reach her in time.

"Ella?" I ask again, my voice soft, gentle.

She looks up at me, and I crouch down, struggling slightly with the movement. I wrap my arms around her and relax as she sinks into me, sobbing gently against my chest.

"I'm scared," she whispers.

"Don't be scared. We're here now. He won't come back." I hold her tight, not letting her go.

"Where has he gone?" Paul asks, looking around him. "Should we phone the police?"

"I think we should," I reply. "He's clearly close by and has been watching us again.

"No," Ella suddenly begs. "You can't!"

"Why?" Beth asks, her face full of confusion. "He's hurt you, Ella. We need to report this."

Ella gestures to the side of the cliff, and Paul walks over to it before gasping audibly. "Shit!"

Beth moves to join Paul and pales as she turns around to face us. She makes the motion of swiping a knife across someone's neck, and I know he's dead.

"Come on, Ella, let's get you away from here," I say as gently as I can manage. She doesn't look like she's capable of moving anywhere, but the only thing running through my mind is the need to get her somewhere safe.

Jess steps up and places one arm around Ella's waist while I hold on to her other side. We take slow and steady steps back to her cottage, Jess carrying most of her weight as we shuffle along in silence. As we reach the doorstep, Jess bends down to remove Ella's shoes before guiding her through her living room and into her bedroom.

The silence stretches between us, only broken now and then by Ella's muffled sobs. I help Ella down onto her bed, and Jess drapes the quilt her mum had made for her around her shoulders before tucking it tight. She leaves us alone together and heads back outside.

I almost want to lie down and close my eyes. Despite only walking a short distance, I'm out of breath, and my forehead feels all clammy, but I force myself to stay sitting. Ella needs me, and I can push through the pain.

"Ella?"

She looks up at me, and her face is empty, drained of the joy that usually fills it. I know she's in shock – I've been there myself.

"Talk to me. What happened?" I whisper as kindly as possible. "You don't need to be afraid anymore. No one can hurt you now."

Ella takes a deep shuddering breath before leaning into me and weeping quietly while clutching my hand tightly in hers.

I stroke circles on her back with my free left hand, feeling all sorts of emotions bubbling inside me; anger that anyone could do this to someone so lovely, guilt for not being able to protect her better today, relief that he is dead and can't hurt her anymore, worry about what will happen to her now.

Her voice is barely a whisper as she speaks, and I hold her close so that I can make out what she's saying.

"I didn't mean to kill him. I had no choice. It was him or me."

"Shh," I say to her. "The police will know it was self-defence. Look at you; you're covered in marks. They know his history and what he's capable of. You're fortunate to have escaped this."

"What if they don't believe me?" she sobs.

I wish I could take all of this hurt away, but I can't promise her things I don't know the answer to. I pause momentarily before squeezing her hand gently and pulling away slightly to look into her eyes.

"We were all witnesses, Ella. Tell us what happened, and we will back up your story." I press a gentle kiss against the top of her head. "We'll make sure it's taken care of."

She nods but doesn't say any more. Instead, she leans her head on my shoulder and lets me hold her close.

Jess re-enters the room a few minutes later, followed by Paul and Beth. My best friends are still in their wedding outfits, and it's hard to believe they got married just an hour ago.

"What's the plan?" Beth asks, her voice calm but firm. "If we're going to phone the police, we need to do it soon. They'll be able to tell what time he died, and we don't want to be seen to be trying to cover anything up."

"We'll call them," I say, gingerly pulling my phone out of my pocket. "We stick to the truth, ok? We all saw what happened. Leonard attacked Ella, we heard her screams, and before we could reach her, he lost his footing and fell over the cliff. Ella was lucky he didn't take her with him."

Jess passes Ella a glass of water and helps her take a sip before handing her a tissue. She's oddly quiet. She's likely in shock too.

"Yes mate, me and Beth definitely saw all of that, didn't we babe?"

"Yeah," Beth replies.

I leave Ella with Jess and move into the front room to make the call. As I dial the emergency number for the police, my thoughts drift back to what Ella had said before. *I didn't mean to kill him. I had no choice. It was him or me.* The words replay in my mind, and I can't help but feel a deep sense of sadness for Ella but also pride in the woman she has become.

She had been pushed to the brink, forced to defend herself against someone who had already hurt her in so many ways yet come out on top. She's a survivor. Seeing what she's capable of dealing with cements in my mind that I can do the same. I can handle nine more weeks, and there's no way I'm leaving more sorrow behind for my girl to deal with.

"The police are on their way," I say as I re-enter the bedroom. "You two should go to your wedding reception. All of your guests will be waiting for you."

"I'm not sure I want to go there now," Beth says, worry lining her features. I catch her eye and shake my head. "You need to go, Beth. You can't let this ruin your day."

Jess nods in agreement. "We'll stay with Ella until the police arrive. You go celebrate with your guests."

Reluctantly, Beth nods and stands up, adjusting her dress. "Okay. But call us if you need anything."

Once they're gone, Jess turns to me and finally speaks. "What's going to happen now?"

"I don't know," I reply honestly. "But nothing and no one will hurt Ella again."

I FEEL REALLY weak as the police get here, their sirens alerting us of their arrival, and I'm almost relieved when Jess offers to answer the door to them so I don't have to stand up again. I'm no longer out of breath, but my body aches all over like I've got the flu, and despite wanting to be here for Ella, I'm struggling to keep propping her up when my own body is collapsing.

Before I can try and get myself more comfortable, we have company. Jess re-enters the bedroom, followed by PCs Pritchard and Bowen. I look up at them as they assess the situation.

"Can I speak to Ella alone?" PC Pritchard asks, and I nod, needing to get a drink and lie down. I kiss Ella gently on the cheek and follow PC Bowen and Jess out of the room.

The front door has been left open, and as I walk through to her living room, I see three police cars parked outside and an ambulance just behind them. They'll probably need the coast guard to get his body safely off the rocks; that or the fire service.

I join Jess and PC Bowen in Ella's front room, but I'm struggling. My head is pounding, and I'm nauseous, mood swings hitting me in waves.

"I'm going to need to take a statement from each of you," the police officer says, and my eyes struggle to focus as he pulls a pen and pad from his uniform. Slowly but surely, exhaustion begins to creep over every inch of my being until I'm struggling to hear anything being said.

"James, are you ok?" Jess asks, shaking me.

I try to snap out of it and refocus on the room, but it's spinning, and I'm having to try hard not to throw up. "Sorry. Not feeling great," I reply, forcing a couple of deep breaths into my lungs.

"He's got cancer," she says to the policeman, talking about me as though I'm not capable of my speech.

"I'll take your statement when you're feeling more up to it," he says as he moves to stand. "Give the station a call when you're ready."

A minute later, I hear more sirens getting closer before a second ambulance arrives. The paramedics enter the cottage without knocking and head straight for the bedroom, where Ella is still sitting with the female police officer.

I try to remain alert so that I know what's going on. I need to be there for my girl like she has been for me. But it's too much.

"Jess? What's going on?" I murmur.

"They're going to take Ella to the hospital, I think. She needs checking over, and they'll want to take evidence before she showers or anything."

"Is she ok?" I say, the desperation evident in my voice.

"She will be," Jess promises me. "I'll go with her. You stay here and rest. Give me your number, and I'll call you as soon as I know what's happening."

I pass her my phone, and she dials her own number so that she has mine. A few minutes later, Ella is led through the front room and out to the ambulance, the quilt her mum made for her still draped around her shoulders, providing the comfort I'm unable to right now.

"I love you," I whisper as she catches my eye, and she smiles sadly in response.

As soon as they all vacate the house, I close my eyes and succumb to exhaustion.

29

ELLA

THREE MONTHS LATER

"It's so great to be back doing this again," Beth exclaims, a look of absolute jubilation on her face. "It feels like forever since we all sat in here together. The Fisherman's Friends reunited!"

I can't help but laugh. "I have high hopes for a second victory," I say, squeezing James' arm as we wait to order our drinks at the bar. He turns to me and smiles, and I can't help but lean in and kiss him. My handsome knight in shining armour.

We'd come for the pub quiz to celebrate, to mark James' achievement of completing his gruelling three final chemo sessions. Everyone who had been supporting him was there, including Jess, who was practically living with us now while she sorted herself out. I couldn't be more proud of him.

"I'll go and grab some seats," Beth says, not waiting for any of us to reply, and I watch as she walks to our usual table near the window, a glass of white wine in her hand.

"What are you drinking?" James asks me, and it takes me less than a second to answer champagne.

"We're celebrating," I tell him. "Celebrating you being cancer free and now completely ready to spend the rest of your life with me!"

"We don't know that for certain," he chuckles. "But I am hopeful. And I only have you guys to thank for that."

He orders a bottle of champagne and five glasses, and I help him carry them to the table. Paul and Jess have already joined Beth, and we slide into the seats at the end.

The Stag's Head is busy now, much busier than it was when I first visited for the pub quiz, but I guess that's what happens to seaside towns in the summer months. The locals disappear among the tourists until it's hard to recognise anyone you know. Still, it's nice to see so many happy people enjoying themselves.

"Turn your phones off and get your pencils and paper ready."

Ah, the familiar sound of Graham, the quizmaster.

"The quiz will be starting in five minutes."

I turn my phone off, not really sure why I brought it with me in the first place. The only people who contact me these days are all sitting around this table, and it is utter bliss. Notifications are overrated.

James smiles at me as I slide my phone back into my pocket and takes my hand. "Thank you," he whispers, so only I can hear him.

"For what?" I reply, and he squeezes my hand tightly.

"For everything. You really don't know how amazing you are, Ella Park."

A blush creeps up my cheeks, and my heart swells with love for this man. "Stop it; you're making me blush," I say, squeezing his hand back. "But really, James, you're the amazing one. The way you've fought through all of this, it's truly inspiring. I'm just happy to be by your side."

He leans in and kisses me softly and sweetly. It's moments like these that remind me how lucky I am to have found someone like him.

"Oi, love birds," Beth laughs. "We're trying to come up with a new quiz team name seeing as there's only actually one working fisherman still sitting around this table."

"Hey, I'll be back on the boat by the end of the season," James laughs. "Just you watch me!"

"How about The Chemo Warriors?" Jess suggests. "In honour of James' battle."

"I like it," I say. "To the Chemo Warriors. Cheers!"

We all raise our glasses before clinking them together in a loud toast. "To James!"

As the night wears on and the champagne flows, I feel a strange sense of contentment settle over me. For the first time in a long time, everything feels right. James is healthy and happy, my stalker is dead, and I feel like I'm exactly where I should be - in this place, with my favourite people by my side.

The quiz comes to a close before we know it, and Jess takes our paper to the bar so that they can tally up the scores. Our anticipation is high for our first quiz in months, but we end up coming in second place. We groan loudly, but it hardly dampens our spirits. Nothing will do that. Not now. Not ever.

Paul and Beth give us both a long hug, their eyes glistening with happy tears as we say our goodbyes. I slip my hand into James', our fingers entwined, as we stroll out of the pub. Jess walks close on our heels, wrapped up in her own thoughts, the same as she'd been for much of the past few weeks.

"Are you ok?" I ask her as James flags a taxi down.

"Yeah, just tired," she replies, giving me a weak smile.

I slip my arm through hers and walk to the taxi with her before enjoying the comfortable silence shared on the short ride home.

I RISE JUST BEFORE DAWN, determined to make today special for James. He has his final oncology appointment today, and I want to make sure he knows how much love and support he has from his friends and me. So, while he takes a shower, I set to work in the kitchen.

I preheat a pan and gather all the necessary ingredients to prepare another speciality of mine - homemade pancakes. I mix all the ingredients together before pouring the mix into the hot fat of the pan. Varying sizes of pancake batter bubble away while I slowly drizzle sticky-sweet maple syrup over the top. James still struggles to taste certain foods due to the chemotherapy, but thanks to a stroke of luck, his ability to taste sweet things hasn't changed. It's been one small comfort in a difficult few months.

I serve the pancakes onto two plates just as he walks out of the shower, a towel tied around his waist. Droplets of water roll down his back, arousing a deep desire inside me to take him back into the bedroom. Unfortunately, a quick look at the clock on the wall tells me we don't have time. Tonight though...

"Oh, Ella, you didn't have to go to all this effort for me," James says as he joins me at the kitchen counter and hops up onto one of the stools.

"Of course I did! Today is officially the first day of the rest of your life. I'm sure of it," I promise. And I am sure of it. He's looking healthier than I've seen him in months. There's no way the oncologist is going to give him bad news today. "Are you sure you don't want me to accompany you?"

"No," he replies. "Honestly. I made you a promise that I would get through the chemotherapy and that you would start writing again. My treatment is over, and you still have one last chapter to write in your novel. I want to read it when I'm home."

A wicked smile forms on my lips, and I know just how I'm going to finish my story. Our story.

"Okay," I chuckle. "I'll make sure it's done before you're home."

I WAVE James off at the door and wish him all the luck in the world before pulling out the gorgeous typewriter he bought for me and setting it up on the living room table. It's been such a great gift, and I can't help but feel inspired every time I use it. Of course, being stalker-free and having James here helps heaps too.

I re-read the last chapter I wrote and then begin typing the finale, the words flowing out of me effortlessly as I describe the end of our story, or perhaps, the beginning of our new one.

JAMES, the warrior that he is, has conquered cancer, and we decide to celebrate this special occasion by taking a trip out to sea on our boat (fictional Ella and James are rich enough to afford a yacht). The sun glints off the water, casting a golden hue over everything as we sail away into the horizon together, more in love than ever before.

We spend the whole day swimming and partying, wrapped up in our own little bubble, not needing anybody else. And as the sun begins to set over the ocean, Ella gets down onto one knee and proposes to the only man she can imagine spending the rest of her life with.

James looks at Ella in utter shock, his eyes widening as she pulls out a small velvet box. He nods his head, tears building in his eyes, as she opens it to reveal a stunning diamond ring. The sunlight catches the diamond, and it sparkles beautifully in the fading light.

"Ella..." James says, his voice shaking with emotion. "Yes! Yes, I will marry you."

Ella throws her arms around James, kissing him deeply, the salty sea air whipping around them as the boat rocks gently on the ocean. Tears of happiness stream down her face as they both laugh and cry in a joyous embrace. Ella slips the ring onto James' finger, the weight of the metal a symbol of their commitment to each other. Now, and forever in the future. THE END.

I FINISH TYPING the last words in my novel and realise I have tears running down my face. The last few months have been such a whirlwind of emotion, but I wouldn't be who I am today if I hadn't gone through everything that happened. And I wouldn't have found the love of my life either.

I hit the print button on my typewriter and grab the neatly stacked pages, my heart thumping in anticipation. The familiar sound of his car rumbling up the drive, followed by the sound of a door slamming shut, tells me that he's finally home. I rush to the door and open it wide, hoping for good news.

"I'm all clear," he shouts, a massive smile on his face as he runs up the path to my cottage.

"I knew it!" I reply. I run towards him and leap into his arms, planting a kiss firmly on his lips. I can taste his joy and relief mingled with the salt of his tears. My heart swells with happiness and gratitude for the universe finally granting us a break. We hold each other tight, not wanting to let go. And then I remember the pages in my hand.

"James, I finished it," I say, handing him the manuscript. "It's our story. I want you to read it."

He takes it from me and studies the cover for a moment. And then he looks up at me with a glimmer in his eyes that I've never seen before. "Read the last chapter to me," he says.

We both take a seat on the picnic bench outside the cottage, not wanting to disturb Jess, and I begin to read the final paragraphs. As I finish the last page, I notice James has moved. He's no longer sitting across from me at the table. He's kneeling next to me, a ring in his hand.

"Ella, you are the love of my life," he says, his voice barely above a whisper. "I know we've been through so much in the short space of time we've known each other, but every moment has been worth it because it brought me closer to you. I want to spend the rest of my life by your side. Will you marry me?"

The ring he holds out is breathtaking; a perfect ruby set in shimmering platinum. My heart races as I look into his eyes, seeing nothing but love and sincerity.

"Yes, James," I say, barely able to keep my voice steady. "I can't think of anything I want more."

EPILOGUE

JESS

I cast a long, slender shadow as I trudge across the cliff to the place where Ella had taken Leonard's life. The horizon is painted with pinks and oranges while the sun slowly sinks below it. Even though three months have passed, I'm still unable to shake the image of Leonard lying there on the ground, lifeless, blood pooling underneath him. Tears roll down my face as I think about everything he sacrificed. I'd told Ella I was only at her cottage that day because I wanted to return her messages in person. But that wasn't exactly the truth.

I'd come here with Leonard that day. I knew what he was about to do, and I was going to stand by and let it happen. She deserved it. It was only when things went south that I had to come up with a Plan B.

I lay a solitary rose at the edge of the cliff as I struggle to wipe away the tears. Grief consumes me. Leonard had been my one true love. We'd dated for a while when I was a teenager and even lived together in the city for a bit. He'd proven his love to me when he'd dealt with Susie. That bitch had had it coming, and Leonard had been all too willing to step up to the plate on my behalf. He never even mentioned my name when the police caught up to him, and he was sent down.

Of course, I'd had to give up our child then. I had no way of caring for him on my own; no way to support myself, let alone a baby.

Leonard hadn't asked me to stick around and wait for him, but I had anyway. Loyalty was rewarded where I came from, and I knew I'd welcome him back into my life as soon as he was released. The ten years in between were spent trying to better my life so I could provide for him the way he had for me.

Ella was a friend at the start, a good one. But when she got her book deal for a novel that didn't take her all that long to write, it made me once again think about everything that is wrong with the world. I'd given her ideas for that book, and she'd never thanked me. Not in public and not in private either. She didn't deserve to become an overnight success. Not while I was spending every waking moment just trying to make ends meet.

The day Leonard was released from prison was the second happiest day of my life; only the day our son was born being better. We were finally together again and could start to build a family. The family I deserved. The family I'd never had growing up.

But Ella was getting on my nerves, and I knew she needed to be dealt with before we could make that happen. Leonard paid the price in the end, but everything he did, he did for me.

I was the one who openly reminisced about this shit hole of a town all the time despite never wanting to lay a foot here ever again.

I was the one who planted the rental listing on the author Discord I knew she visited daily.

I was the one that took the photo of James' letter so that we could emulate it and break them up.

I was the one telling Leonard where she was and who she was with. The doorbell feed being sent to Leonard's phone? That was my doing when I encouraged her to ask for added security.

And when she gave me her old phone, I was able to sync it to her new one and track her every movement.

I did all that. Me. And I did it all while pretending to be the best friend she could ever ask for.

And what did I have to show for it? Nothing. The love of my life was dead, and I was stuck in the spare bedroom of a cottage in a town I hated, having to deal with love's young dream. It made me sick.

I press my hands against the curve of my stomach, conscious of the tiny growing life inside me. We take a walk here every night, the moonlit landscape our only company. But unlike most expectant mothers who whisper sweet promises to their children of the world they are going to grow up in, I tell my son the truth. He's going to grow up knowing exactly what happened to him and exactly who did it.

And then she'll regret it.

THE END

AUTHOR'S NOTE

Writing this book was a true labour of love and I couldn't have done it without the help of some amazing people. The biggest thanks must go to Stephanie, my editor, who gave me so much good advice and helped turn my story into something worth publishing. Her late-night words of wisdom helped me more than she will ever know.

A big thank you also must be given to Rachel, Laura, Kirsty, Aoife and Catie for listening to me talk about this novel for days on end. These fantastic women helped keep me sane while I completed one of the hardest things I've ever done.

Thank you to Tom for checking that my information surrounding James' diagnosis and treatment was accurate, and thank you to Perrin of The Author Buddy for creating the cover for this story.

I also have to thank my best friend, Jess – for just being an all-around badass and having the perfect name – and my husband – who did more than his fair share of childcare duties to enable me to continue writing.

Finally, a massive thank you goes to you, the reader. Choosing to purchase a debut novel from an unknown author is huge! Reading through to the end is an even bigger deal. I really appreciate you picking up this story and giving it a read, and I hope you enjoyed your time with it.

If you'd like to sign up to my mailing list to be notified of future books, you can find it via my website at oliviasnowauthor.com. Reviews are also mean a lot to indie authors like myself, so please do leave one if you enjoyed this book.

Thank you,

Olivia Snow